LUCAS

Copyright

Title book: Lucas

Author book: Richard Alan Meredith

Text copyright © Richard Alan Meredith, 2021

Cover photo copyright © Richard Alan Meredith, 2020

ALL RIGHTS RESERVED. This book contains material protected under International and Federal Copyright Laws and Treaties. Any unauthorized reprint or use of this material is prohibited. No part of this book may be reproduced or transmitted in any form or by any means, electronic or mechanical, including photocopying, recording, or by any information storage and retrieval system without express written permission from Richard Alan Meredith.

Lucas is dedicated to my little brother. You are stronger than you know little bro.

Wednesday, 24th February, 19:03

As sure as day follows night, does repent follow the sin. I'm in A.A. again, the secular version, the Diet Coke version (all the taste with none of the religion). I would happily go to confession if I could get past the narthex. I have heard it said that we are all children of God and none of us should be judged except by the Almighty himself. It's either not true or he has already made his mind up about me.

The strip lights in here are hard and unforgiving, the white walls maximising the effect. The glare is giving me a headache despite the high tint sunglasses I have on. It's also one of the reasons confessionals appeal. No harsh lighting there. Just a curtained box with some candles outside, maybe even a nun. Sounds heavenly!

Despite the chair being one of those metal framed, right angle ones (surely designed for maximum uncomfortableness) I manage to achieve a supine position like I am catching some rays.

Out of the corner of my eye I notice a guy staring, clockwise to me in the circle of trust. What's his deal? He looks disgusted which seems a bit rich considering we are all here for the same reason, well loosely speaking. Maybe he thinks I'm asleep which obviously makes it OK to stare!?#!

I flick open my squinted left eye and announce, "What?"

He jumps. I laugh but have the decorum not to let it reach my mouth. I don't plan on giving up the moral high ground anytime soon.

"Your mouth... your neck... your shirt," he stutters, "It's covered in... something?"

Shit! I forgot to wash up before I decided to come here. A choir boy error but easily explained.

"It's cider and black, it never agrees with me."

"Oh!"

Mystery explained, he loses interest and looks toward the empty seat where our absent group leader should be.

Oh, but the shirt though! I forgot I was wearing it. It's Egyptian cotton and tailored. It doesn't matter what is done to it, the blood will never truly wash out.

The scrape of metal along the tiled floor (almost as excruciating as the lighting) announces the arrival of our glorious leader. To be clear, I am not particularly fond of Nigel. He has the kind of face that should only be a few seconds away from the next slap, his voice has the same melodic appeal as the scraping chair, and he is always late. In any other circumstance I would have happily snapped his neck like a piece of dry spaghetti. His only saving grace is that he is here and that means we can start.

At this point in the proceedings, I am always torn between two poles of excitement. As an extrovert, I can't wait for my chance to perform and regale the group with my latest exploits. However, I take equal pleasure in hearing the reciprocal stories from the other sinners in the group. It almost makes me feel that I am not alone and at least once per meeting, there is pure gold.

Now that I am sat forward in my chair, I notice there are some faces I don't recognise, new blood! I decide to keep my powder dry for the moment. After a few minutes of Nigel prattle, we start properly.

"Hi... *cough*... my name is Dave."

Dave's story is typical. Stressful job -> started drinking -> depression -> drank some more -> partner left -> drank some more -> lost job -> lost flat... boo-hoo! You wouldn't see Clint Eastwood crying, he'd hunt down the first person who gave him a drink and, while the alcohol toting villain cowered at the bottom of the barrel of a large handgun, he'd ask him, "Wanna bet a fiver there's not a bullet in this chamber?"

Clint may not, but God loves a tryer, and so do I. When he concludes, I moderate my clapping down to match the flock which is somewhere between applause for a single run in a village green cricket game or an average tee shot on a Thursday afternoon televised golf game.

There are a couple more 'Daves' & 'Davettes' and each time I clap dutifully whilst conveying a sympathetic face which says without saying, "We've all been there Dave."

Next is Karl. He has short, dark hair which he keeps nervously running his hands through. I have a good feeling about him. Be brave Karl, what's said in the circle of trust stays in the circle.

He stares at the floor, clearly not wanting to meet anyone's eye as he starts, "I know I hit rock bottom when..."

BINGO!

"... I was swaying back and forth outside my front door when I realised, I had lost my keys. I didn't fancy knocking and waking the missus up, so I decided the best course of action would be to climb over the side wall, retrieve the back door key from under the gnome, sneak in quiet like, tip toe up the stairs and deftly slip into bed. No harm, no foul. I clumsily vaulted over the wall but am saved by a cushioning bush on the other side. After I brushed myself down, I weaved along the side and back of the house until I arrived at the back door. I couldn't find the key. I couldn't even find the smug bloody gnome. I did find a ladder though and a new plan came together. Plan C: use the ladder to get onto the extension roof; it was quite a balmy night so I was pretty confident she would have left the window open; sneak in like the Milk Tray Man and; slip straight into bed. On paper this new plan looked better than Plan A (front door entry) or Plan B (back door entry) which both involved creeping through an unlit house. At least this way I would be straight in without even traipsing up the creaky stairs or having to open and close our squeaky bedroom door. Getting up the ladder was harder than I thought it would be and, near the top, I cracked out an enormous fart, loud enough to rattle the glass in the bedroom's window frames. I froze but no lights came on, so I started to think that maybe someone up on high was looking out for me. It wasn't until I was most of the way across the roof that I realised that there was more in my pants than my Tommy Cannon & Bobby Balls. That fart had brought more than the thunder. The summer breeze at my back carried a god-awful smell that confirmed what I suspected, that I had followed through. There was no Plan D or even a Plan P, unless that 'P' stood for 'panic' instead of 'poo'. I immediately started yanking my trousers off, desperate to get rid of my cotton wrapped turd. Somehow, I managed to get my trousers and fragrant pants off without falling off the pitched roof, despite needing to balance one legged to remove the aforementioned garments. At this point my smugness level reached the level of my AWOL gnome. That moment of glory disappeared like a fart in the wind when the light in the bedroom came on, immediately followed by the curtains and window being opened. I was staring uncomprehendingly at old Mrs. Jones from next door, trying to figure out why she was in my house in her dressing gown. I saw her eyes were every bit as wide as mine although she was at eye-to-eye level with Karl Junior. She was so close I could feel her breath on my nethers, and I instinctively took a step back, but my heel got caught in my dropped trousers. I tottered backwards, arms windmilling as I tried to regain my balance. As I fell backwards, I let go of my poo parcel, which at this juncture had gained a few revolutions worth of velocity. The last thing I saw as I pitched off the roof was the perfect launch of my special delivery heading straight for the open-mouthed Mrs. Jones. The next thing I remember was waking up on my neighbour's patio with blue lights filling the sky. Unfortunately for me it was the police rather than the ambulance which took me away. I was charged with indecent exposure and assault with a deadly weapon. The charges were later dropped but not before my missus upped and left."

Reliving this tragic night has clearly depleted Karl, and it is clear that if he had the energy, he would be in tears now. I try my best, but I am human. Well almost human. I howl with laughter like Spike in one of those old Tom & Jerry cartoons. When I finally pull myself together, removing the tears from my eyes with the back of my finger, I see the rest of the group are less than impressed with my outburst. Nigel regards me with a contempt that should be reserved for grown men who soil themselves (sorry Karl, had to be said).

"Lucas, do we have to revisit the rules again? I am not going to divert anymore precious session time on these inappropriate outbursts. Please wait at the end so we can have a chat. In the meantime, do try to control yourself."

I did hang around for that 'chat'. His neck didn't snap like dry spaghetti. It did make some rather satisfying popping noises though, like bursting bubble wrap.

Wednesday, 24th February, 21:15

"Yo Pops, I'm back."

He scampers into the kitchen from the living room, like a trapdoor spider.

"Where the bloody hell have you been? I've been worried sick."

He worries but that is his reason for being. He's like my Alfred the Butler except he really is my dad.

"I don't know why you fret so much, there's nothing worse than me out at night."

"That's the bloody point! You've been gone for two nights which means two days too!"

"We-l-l... the first night I stayed at a mate's..."

"You haven't got any friends Luke."

"Well, you got me there old man but I did stay somewhere with a roof the first night and last night I got caught short and slept in the park."

"The park! You slept in a hole in the park!"

"Of course I buried myself. I wouldn't have slept in a hammock with factor 50 on!"

"Well at least your home now but look at the state of your clothes. That shirt is Egyptian cotton. I don't think I'll be able to get the mud stains out. Maybe if I use some Vanish from under the sink..."

"I had a drink."

The words that Pops was praying I wouldn't say, and they create a heavy silence. Even the cars outside seem to have stopped driving past. There is something cathartic when a parent shouts at you when you have done something wrong, like you instantly start repaying some soul debt. The ashamed driven silence leaves me feeling naked and alone with my guilt. I can't take this vulnerable feeling of exposure. I need his sympathy not his judgement.

"It was an old guy living on the streets. He smelt like feet. He was riddled with cancer, and he didn't have long left. I could sense he was in a lot of pain, and he practically begged me to do it. I made sure it was quick and painless."

Lie, lie, lie, lie, lie, lie, lie and a side order of lies.

She was a vivacious young girl out celebrating her 20th birthday. She was training to be a doctor and so healthy I think she would have lived well past her hundredth birthday. True, she was in no pain until I began to feed and then she begged me to stop. But the bloodlust was upon me, and I lapped up the blood and fear in equal measure. It was as slow and painful as I could have made it. The lie carries a soul debt but insignificant compared to the act it concealed. I lock this episode away in a trunk marked 'DO NOT OPEN' in a dusty yet crowded corner of my mind attic.

The 'C-Bomb' was a low blow though. Pops was diagnosed with cancer when he was 60. He recovered but I knew it was leverage to bring him round.

Pops' frown softens and he is able to look at me again.

"Well, that's something at least. We say it's inhumane to let animals suffer but don't offer the same courtesy to humans. You performed a public service really."

I could dip into his thoughts and see if he really believes what he is saying but decide I'd rather not know.

He shuffles slowly over to the calendar and crosses out 363 (days without a drink) and then writes 2. He looks like death on legs as he makes his way over to the newspaper covered sofa in the lounge. Before his bum manages to make contact with the cushion I shout, "Make us a coffee Pops, I'm going to take a shower."

When I come back downstairs, I sit and watch the soaps with him. Emmerdale, then Corrie and finally Eastenders. Truth to be told, I can't stand them. They're like listening to a 'Lighthouse Family' CD stuck on repeat. Frankly put, Van Gogh music. Vincent Van Gogh cut off his ear whilst hallucinating, during that delusion he could clearly hear 'Ocean Drive' being played on a nearby gramophone. I seem to remember the writers dropped a plane on Emmerdale once, they should have called it quits there and then. I watch dutifully as Pops could do with the company plus, I have found, a knowledge of the soaps can come in useful.

After the soaps we get into some ITV murder mystery. Twenty minutes in, the inevitable happens, and Pops succumbs to sleep. He has an uncanny knack of being able to fall asleep sat up straight. With no pillow to support his head, the weight of it opens his mouth like he is trying to drink rain falling from a cloud. If it wasn't for his bone rattling snore, I am sure he could sleep like that all night. His snore alarm does its job and Pops' head pivots back into a more natural position and his confused eyes take a moment to work out where he is. Half believing he could perform the same trick on his feet (I reckon he could do it too), Pops hurriedly heads for the stairs. He squeezes me on the shoulder as he passes, and I squeeze his hand back.

"Night Luke. See you tomorrow at sundown."

"Night Pops. Love you."

Despite the thickness of the walls in this house, it's only a short intermission before his bedroom turns into a giant speaker, amplifying his guttural breathing.

That's my alarm call. I switch off the TV, carefully lift my keys from the coffee table and slip out the door.

There was no question about where I was going tonight, Las Midas. A bar that serves food during the day, and early evening, but then at night turns into a small club.

I'm perched at the mirrored, bottle lined bar. Nothing stares back at me. No-one notices though. You would have to look for it (everyone's minds are on other things) and even if someone did, they wouldn't believe what they saw (or more precisely, what they didn't see). I'm nursing a JD & Coke (slowly turning the glass watching the ice cubes melt) when my mind catches a thought. I look to my left and there is a non-descript guy playing the same game with his drink. Regardless of anything distinctive he has the air of someone you wouldn't want to mess with.

"You have got to be kidding me!" I cry.

I slap the bar in excitement.

The non-descript guy turns to his right and enquires, "What?"

"What's your name mate?"

"Piss off!"

"No seriously. I bet you fifty quid I can guess."

I reach into my wallet and lay a pristine fifty pound note on the bar and tether it in place with my drink. He gives me the kind of smile that someone may have when they have a king high flush in poker.

"Alright. You've got no fucking chance."

"Game on."

I pick up the note and tear it carefully down the middle. I place one half back under my drink and slip the other under his.

"Let me see... your first name begins with an... S..."

Non-descript guy chuckles and starts to reach for my expensive coaster.

"R!"

His hand stops and his smile falters.

"Rrr... Rrri... no... Reg... Reg... Reginald. Right?"

"Is this some fucking con? Do you know me?"

"No, no con. I can honestly say I have never met you before in my life."

I wait until I am sure he is not going to leave before continuing.

"Reginald... Ru... Rupert...."

The corner of his stubby mouth twitches north.

"No... that's not quite right.... But there's definitely a 'U' in it.... U-U-U-Uri-Uriah!"

He quickly stands up and looms over me looking menacing, but I can detect a hint of fear.

"Calm down. It's just a bit of fun. Look. If you win you get the money. If I win, I just get the satisfaction of winning. Your wallet will be no lighter."

"Okay."

He sits back down but he looks as tense as a sprinter in their starting blocks.

"Last name then. I want to say Ritchie, like the director, but that's not quite right, is it? Itchy! It's 'Itchy' isn't it? Reginald Uriah Itchy. R. U. Itchy. Ah come on, that is brilliant!"

"What the fuck... how did you?"

"Oh, I learnt how to do it from a Derren Brown book. It's not that hard once you learn how to pick up on people's tells. Well, are you?"

"Am I what?"

"Itchy?"

"Fuck off!"

"Well, I know you didn't win the grand prize Reg, but can I buy you a drink for being such a good sport?"

"I'll have a double Jameson with ice. Remind me never to play cards with you. What's your name?"

"Indeed. Lucas."

I get the barman's attention and order Reg's drink.

"So, what do you do for a living Reg?"

"I'm a budgie smuggler."

I spit JD & coke all over my section of the bar and a little on the barman who gives me a look.

"Pardon me. I choked on an ice cube there. Did you say you were a budgie smuggler?"

"Yep. Well, any type of exotic bird really: parrots; cockatoos... I don't usually tell people what I do but you are clearly someone who could smell a lie, plus people with a dark side don't usually judge. And you look like you have one."

"Looks like I am not the only one who can read others."

Reg immediately downs his double whiskey and, after an indistinct thanks, leaves.

I am still sniggering to myself when a young and attractive woman occupies Reg's still warm bar stool. She has a tight, low-cut top on, which fully exposes her shoulders and neck.

She smiles at me with perfectly white teeth and asks, "Would you like a drink?"

I flash a smile back and reply, "Yes, like you wouldn't believe."

Thursday, 25th February, 23:15

Another night, another bar. I can't be seen in the same place with a soon to be missing girl on my arm each night. I am at one of my least favourite fishing holes, 'Jupiter'. I set up in my usual location, perched at the bar nursing a JD & Coke. However, my upper back and shoulders are highly tensed as the unnecessarily loud dance music mercilessly pounds the back of my head. In my warm life I would have avoided this place like the plague. Despite this I want... scratch that... need a drink and this place is a good bet.

No one is going to approach me in here with the body language I am emitting so I spin round, slide off the stool and go for a wander. The stroll does nothing for my headache as I have to skirt the even noisier dance floor looking for potentials. It's next to impossible to concentrate while being rhythmically sound punched and simultaneously blink blinded by the light show.

I escape to a fractionally quieter corner at the back of the club to gather my thoughts. I have one thought which repeats on every percussion beat, "GET-OUT, GET-OUT, GET-OUT, GET-OUT..." OK, I give in. I will have to settle for fast food tonight.

On what feels like a Lord of the Rings-esque trek to the exit, I spot a bored looking girl waiting for her boyfriend to stow his coat in the cloakroom. She's not my usual taste but I could see how a lot of men who would find her attractive, underlined by how little clothing she has on (just a short skirt and a bra top). Based on how I currently feel this will be an advantage, nothing to unwrap.

"You'll do," I huff as I lead her by the hand back out of the club. She follows willingly enough with a modicum of mind manipulation (impressive even by my standards). I don't think the boyfriend realised what happened as he had his back to us the whole time. It was as easy as snatching a mobile phone out of his back pocket, very careless of him.

I stride towards the nearest alleyway, leading my quarry gently by the hand. She trots as best she can in her high heels to keep up. The alley swallows us whole, and I quickly find us a more secluded spot behind some commercial bins. Against the wall her head lolls to one side, exposing her neck. She looks up at me with space cadet eyes. She is being very compliant. On reflection, maybe I put the whammy on her too hard. I crouch down to drink (even with the impossible heels she is damn short) but I am forced to pause. How much perfume has she got on? Jesus! That's more effective than a garland of garlic or l'eaux saintes. How many of my senses are going to be assaulted tonight? With a face like I am eating something gross as a dare, I move in and bite down.

It's not long before we are rudely interrupted.

"Get the fuck off her!"

Ah shit! Another rooster in the hen house. The boyfriend, n'est-ce pas? I let my scantily clad acquaintance collapse sideways, onto the soft landing of some binbags, as I stagger into the middle of the alley to face the music.

The boyfriend looks furious and, bless him, he's brought some friends too! They are a couple of big slabs of meat. Shoulder to shoulder they fill the alleyway. I am guessing that is their purpose, stopping me from escaping. In contrast to his half naked girlfriend, badass boyfriend is covered up in a long, black leather coat. Minus some shades and he looks like a 'Blade' cosplayer. Maybe I am in trouble.

I give a little wave and say politely, "Evening."

My warmth does not defrost the tension. He points to a spot behind me and snarls, "That's mine."

I look to where his girlfriend is taking a nap and turn my head back to face forwards. The whole alley moves like we are in the middle of an earthquake. Somehow, the tremor only affects me, and I stumble, whilst my uninvited guest appears rooted to the ground like a Treeman. What the hell is wrong with me?

The acrid taste in my mouth sparks a thought in my befuddled brain.

"Pardon me sir, if it's not too personal a question. Are you a drug dealer?"

"Are you fuckin' serious? You piss off with my girl to fuck her behind some bins and now you want to buy some drugs from me?"

"To be honest with you, I've probably had as much as I can handle for one night. I might go and sit on those bags with your missus before I fall over. They look comfy."

"Right then funny man, first I am going to fuck you up and then it's her turn."

I look back again at 'her' and see her mangled neck. I turn back to retort which causes another quake. I hold my hands out to the side, and spread my feet, in an effort to stay standing. When I am confident, I am not going to topple I respond, "Not intending to upset you further, but if that is what you are looking forward to, then you may be a tad late."

'Blade' reaches into his coat and pulls out a gun. I see the point of the long leather coat now, stylish yet functional. He could probably get away with hiding a shotgun in there, or a sword.

Anyway, this situation had already spiralled out of control. What is required here is a measure of diplomacy.

"Again, no offence intended, but my Pops always told me that cowards carry guns. Show's you are too afraid to stand toe to toe with a geezer."

BANG!

I totter backwards and end up falling next to the missus. Her glassy, lifeless eyes stare into mine.

He shot me! Was it something I said, or did? Maybe both? That was never going to kill me unless he was packing hollow-points, but it hurt every bit as much as it would have in my warm life. The pain is useful though. It sharpens my mind and the world stops spinning. That's when I notice her wrists. There was an attempt to cover up deep purple bruises with concealer. The heavy makeup may not have been a style choice after all, but more of means to hide the black eyes underneath. In my haste I didn't notice any of this before, or the silver bracelet which spelled out the name 'Amber' in cursive text. I reckon if I looked under her skirt, I would see bruises there too. I slip back into feeling like a human again. Sometimes my human side makes a rare appearance. Like I needed any more ammunition to do this motherfucker damage. I get to my feet.

BANG!

The bullet passes through my left breast and makes a mess exiting my upper back. I don't fall back this time; in fact, it doesn't even break my stride.

BANG! 3 steps away...

BANG! 2 steps away...

BANG! 1 step away...

He didn't miss once, but now we are standing toe to toe.

"Are you ready for that fist fight now?"

"What the f…"

"Ding – ding!"

"Ding what?"

"It means the bell has sounded for round one."

I think he would have said "What?" again if I hadn't twatted him. His head rotates on his neck so that he is staring permanently backward toward his large chums, his slack jaw now only attached by a bag of skin. He falls backwards (or is it forwards as he is now facing that way) at the feet of the human wall. I'm not sure if he is dead or paralysed (kind of hoping for the latter). Either way, it's too much for the roid brothers and they beat a hasty retreat out of the alley, moving faster than I would have given either credit for.

I grab the sleeve of the drug dealer's jacket and pull. It comes off as he rolls helplessly, face first into puddle. Well, he is defo going to die now once he finishes his impression of a SodaStream. I return to the back of the alley and place the coat over the girl. It would be like tucking her up into bed if I hadn't needed to pull it over her head.

I zig zag to the front of the alley although I have every intention of walking in a straight line. I need to get home. When I reach the street, I turn right and stagger in the opposite direction to the way back.

Friday, 26th February, 20:30

The problem with getting shot is that it makes you really hungry. Did I satisfy that hunger by taking down bad guys and putting the terminally ill out of their misery? If that makes you feel more comfortable then please believe the beautiful lie. The truth is that I am very picky when it comes to what I eat. Ask any Michelin star chef, persons of taste eat with their eyes and nose first. Putting smell to one side, that's just basic food hygiene, I only feed from beautiful women. This is the part where you decide I am incredibly shallow (parked alongside a few other judgements you have made along the way) but try to suspend your prejudice until I have had an opportunity to explain. When I say beautiful, I don't mean lookalikes for the Sports Illustrated Swimsuit Edition or FHM's 100 Sexiest Women. That's not to say I haven't fed from some women who (prior to meeting me) would not have looked fabulous in a photo shoot but, what I am getting at is, it is the beauty which shines through the surface, directly from someone's soul that counts. Now some of those unmodelike women you may pass in the street, you may not even give them a second glance, but get stuck in a lift with them, and get talking, and you are almost blinded by the exquisiteness of their very essence. I am talking about the spark that existed well before the vessel was created. In my warm life I was never a big wine drinker, but I understood the principle of a fine wine versus a five pound bottle of plonk.

So, put more succinctly, I only drink fine wine. As to why, "only girls?", I would struggle to put my finger on that. Maybe I just like the look of the bottles more.

I have been around the block too many times to be surprised by much. I see a lot of the same stuff orbiting in smaller or larger cycles. Having said that I almost fall off my bar stool when I meet Tyler.

He looks like he has seen too much life to be twenty but too young to be forty (but in reality he could be anywhere in between), six feet tall, slim and sporting the slickest of suits with a white T-shirt underneath. I am sure, if he wanted to, he could star in a designer aftershave commercial, but to be frank, with what he is emitting from his core, he could have fallen out the ugly tree and hit every branch on the way down and he still would have shone. In fact, sitting next to him is like being bathed in gloriously warm, golden sunlight. I should have been scared but, quite the opposite, I am close to euphoria.

It was too tempting not to dip into his thoughts. Well, I intended to dip but it was like I fell from the continental shelf with heavy weights tied to my ankles. I get up off the floor and dust myself down. I am outside the shell of a burnt-out house. The front door is boarded up. Intrigued, I pull off the boards to reveal a blackened front door. Out of place, there is a pristine brass (no, surely gold) plate fixed upon it. It reads,

CASA DE TYLER
KEEP OUT!

So naturally I open the door and step through.

The interior of the house is not quite what I expect. In fact, the interior is the exterior. I step out onto finely manicured grass (like a golf fairway or a middle-class garden where the husband does every maintenance job under the sun to avoid spending anytime with his wife who equally keeps the kitchen to hospital levels of cleanliness). On either side of me are tall (above head height), thick hedges cut with perpendicular precision. I turn back to see the door has gone, replaced with the same unnatural natural order. I start walking until I reach a gap in the hedge to my right. My directional choices have increased from two to three. I peer around the end of the gap and see another identical view. I'm in a bloody maze! Just like the one in the Overlook Hotel.

I've been lost in here for hours, although it feels like days. In frustration, I even tried to push my way through the hedge to achieve a straight trajectory, but it was no good. The branches were so dense it was like trying to push through high density foam, apart from the scratches I received for my efforts. In fact, when I found the pond, I thought it was a mirage (as though my mind could not cope with the despair of seeing another identical hedge lined avenue).

It's not a common garden pond. It's a large stone affair about four metres in diameter, covered in lichen which gives it an appearance of age. In the middle of the pond there are three enormous statues standing back-to-back. They are three giant lizards perched on their tails (I am not even sure any species of lizard can do that) and gallons of water are pouring out of their gaping mouths. I peer into the pond. It's deep and dark, not at all what I was expecting. I assumed it would be like those ornamental ponds you find at garden centres that people through coins into. This one does appear to have that in common, as I can see a metallic glint at the bottom of the murky depths. What is that? I lean forward over the pool to get a better look, as I attempt to see past the distracting constant movement of the water's surface.

If you asked me if I was pushed or sucked in, I would find it impossible to say for sure, but I suddenly find myself rushing headlong into the water as if I had dived. I am a body length under the water before I get my bearings. I can definitely see something shiny, partially uncovered in the pond's bed. Curious I swim downwards to investigate. As I get closer, I am better able to discern its shape. Is that a gun? My fingertips make contact with the cold metal and my eyes are blinded by a white flash.

The colour bleeds back in and I find myself sat in a puddle of pond water outside of a pair of large, black, wrought iron gates. I stand up and flap my arms twice to shake off some of the water absorbed by my clothes. The right-hand gate is open with a mangled padlock hanging off it. Despite the words 'Keep Out', 'Warning' and 'Danger' being repeated in twisted iron lettering throughout the structure of the gates, I squelch forward into the graveyard beyond.

The graveyard is immense and after walking a short time, I am as lost as I was in the maze. All the headstones are of identical height, style and all are etched with words I can't read. I don't even recognise the characters. They may be Chinese, Russian or some long dead language. At the hundredth... scratch that... the thousandth stone, the unintelligible letters come to life and start to move around like serpents until they settle upon some text I can understand:

LOOKING FOR ANSWERS?
LOOKING FOR MEANING?
YOU MUST DIG FOR THE TRUTH
TO SEEK YOUR HEART'S HEALING

The clatter of an unnoticed spade falling from its propped position on the headstone makes me jump. I've come this far. I pick it up and start digging.

When I reach about six feet below ground the spade twangs and vibrates in my hands as metal to metal contact is made. I drop to my knees and brush the earth away from the epicentre of the contact. A bit more hand excavation later and I reveal a hatch. I open it and lower myself through. I let go when I realise the drop is only a few feet.

I find myself in a lift. It's a bog-standard lift as you would find in any tall building, or car park, apart from the control panel whose numbering looks more like a chronology rather than depicting floor levels. I pick the lowest on the list, 1990, thinking I must be currently at the top. The lift drops like a stone, and it leaves my stomach where I started. I don't know how fast the lift is travelling, but surely anything this fast should come with seat belts and a sick bag. The lift decelerates as quickly as it accelerated, and my stomach returns with a strong recommendation to empty itself. I am on all fours and manage only to allow spit to exit my mouth. I get unsteadily to my feet and blink in an effort to regain my bearings. The lift appears to be dead. Maybe I am between floors? I press the button which shows a diagram of the doors opening. Big mistake! As they open, earth starts pouring into the carriage. Within a short space of time, I will be buried in this metal trap. Although my legs are already stuck, I manage to reach the control panel and push the 'doors closed' button. Clearly this is no ordinary lift, and its doors are of the same calibre, they close as if there was no impediment at all. Just before the doors close fully, a metal lunchbox tumbles in on the last of the moving earth. It's faded and rusty but clearly a bit of merchandise from the cartoon version of 'Beetlejuice'. It also very misshapen, like it has been bashed about. It hasn't received any external blows though, any impacts appear to have originated from inside the box.

The lunchbox jumps in my hands. I follow suit which makes this the second time in a long time that something has made me do that (the gun shots I took in the last act did make me jump for a different reason, they don't count). The box leaps in my hands again unexpectedly, and I almost drop it. My curiosity outweighs my jitters and I open the clasp on the side.

The lizard is out and launching itself at me before I can do much else other than drop the box and try to get back out of harm's way (quite difficult when you are waist deep in dirt). Its mouth is wide open and all I can see are gold serrated teeth primed to close like a bear trap.

S-H-H-I-I-T......

I do fall off the bar stool this time. Tyler appears in the top left of my field of vision which is currently taking in the ceiling for the first time, although I have been to this bar many times. He doesn't look best pleased.

"I don't know what you are, but I have had my fill of you otherworldly creatures. Now listen, if you enter my private space again, I won't stop him next time. Do you un-der-stand?"

The last three syllables are said individually, as if I am simple or hard of hearing. I am still too stunned to move, but at least my mouth still works, "Understood."

Tyler leaves stage left and is replaced with a brick shit house of a bouncer.

"Had too much sir?"

"Yes, I rather think I have had more than I can handle for one evening."

I walk aimlessly through town after being forcibly ejected from the bar. The bald bouncer did me a favour by hoisting me to my feet, as I was not one hundred percent sure I could stand prior to this. Kill or cure as they say. I am still dazed by tonight's events. As I said I am rarely surprised by something new. So, lost in my thoughts I fail to notice the hooded teenage girl until she blocks my path.

"I'll give you whatever you want for twenty quid."

The tremble in my hand reminds me why I was out again tonight.

"I rather think you are overselling yourself my dear, but let's see what you've got."

Sunday, 27th February, 01:12

I don't count smoking as one my vices. I didn't smoke in my warm life. I hate the smell, the way it clings to your clothes, hair and skin. So why, you may ask, am I leisurely puffing on a Marlborough Light with the rest of the pack keeping kindred company with a lighter in my back pocket? And the answer is... the Angler Fish! For those of you who think there are no other fish other than those you can buy battered in the fish & chip shop, allow me to enlighten you. The Angler Fish lives in the deepest, therefore darkest, depths of the ocean. It's a predator with the nastiest set of teeth outside, or inside, Fangoria's movie of the week. If you were unfortunate enough to have it clamp onto your hand, removing it would leave nothing but serrated bone. The 'Alcatraz' teeth are part of an evolutionary set up that ensures that the scant prey, which lives that far down, doesn't get away if it happens upon this monster in the dark. Apart from the scarcity of food, the other key disadvantage of living at this depth, is that you can't see a fin in front of your face. Fish supper could be just a few metres away and you wouldn't know. Not that this is a problem for the Angler Fish, as he knows how to advertise. He has a growth, which extends out from between his eyes, ending in a small bulb. Using bio luminescence, it lights up like a lonely streetlamp in the darkness, advertising to lesser predators that there is an easy meal on offer. How ironic! When a fish comes to investigate and comes within striking distance of the Angler Fish's barbed cavern of a mouth, it's game over. So, the moral of the tail, is that there is no point having the best teeth in the business if you haven't got an audience. Now, I have many talents, but bio luminescence is not one of them, so here I stand in the mouth of a dark alley, advertising my presence with an artificial orange glow that lies at the end of a cigarette.

A woman in her late teens with glasses on (I don't know why but I love glasses) approaches me and I don't need to skim her thoughts to know what she wants.

Just out of reach from someone with normal reflexes she asks, "Can I have a cigarette?"

In a well-practised, quick and fluid movement, I cover her mouth before she can scream and drag her behind the dark shroud of the alley behind me. The tobacco fuelled neon sign fizzles and dies as it lands in a nearby puddle.

"Pops? What are you doing?"

He hasn't woken me up since my long gone school days and he certainly never used this method. He's knelt, astride my chest so that his knees are pinning my arms to my sides. He's leant forward upon a sharpened stake, placed precisely in a gap between my rib bones. The skin is punctured, and the tip is about half way through the rib meat. A fraction more weight applied, or if I try to buck him, and he is going to score a bullseye. He's holding back his full body weight, but when that changes, it's going to be game over. I can feel his heart rate, double what it should be, vibrating through the stake. It almost feels like my heart is beating again. There are beads of sweat running down his face (hope they don't land on me) and his eyes are as wild as his silver hair which looks like there is a current running through it.

"I know what you've done."

He's going to have to be more specific than that. If I do a 'Goonie-esque' Chunk confession Pops is going to get a cramp in one of his thighs before I finish. Plus, I am not going to own up to anything unless I have to.

"The girls Luke! The girls!" he shouts with anguish, as spittle lands on my face.

Seems I am not going to escape being hit by Pops' bodily fluid after all. The outburst causes the stake to move forward a fraction.

He motions to my left with his head and spread out on the floor are copies of the South Wales Echo from the last five days. I recognise the faces of all the dead girls on each of the front pages. I remember with distinct clarity how each of them tasted.

"I should have done this years ago Luke, but you promised, you promised it wouldn't happen again. Those poor girls."

It's easy to switch gears seamlessly from guilt to anger. Especially when rage is never far from the surface.

"DO IT OLD MAN! You are absolutely spot on. You should have done this years ago. That way, neither of us would have had this river of blood trailing behind us. You're the parent. You're supposed to do what's best for me. SO FUCKING WELL DO IT ALREADY!!!"

I can no longer feel his heartbeat over the vibration of his whole body, which is now shaking. He releases the pressure on the stake slightly as he sets himself to push it home. I dip into his thoughts and see the world through Pops' eyes. I am still below him but not as I am now. I am a baby, a defenceless child staring up at him. The age I was when Mum left. He's like Robocop fighting his classified directive 4, preventing him from doing what needs to be done. Looks like he is also going to fail to comply with directive 2 in the process.

The pressure on my chest releases as he falls sideways onto the papers and curls up into a ball sobbing. In one fluid movement I get to my feet and look down at his prone, spasming form.

Pops used to be a lion man. John Wayne, Burt Reynolds and Clint Eastwood genetically engineered into one man. He never backed down to anyone, even if they were twice his size. I remember there was this guy Pops used to know called Don Breaker. The man was a mountain, a farmer type with forearms as big as Pops' waist. I remember he had these Irish Wolf Hounds, as big as horses, but next to him they just looked like ordinary dogs. Now Don suspected Pops of tucking him up on a deal, skimming some extra off the top and not sharing. Pops held his nerve, stuck to his story, and stared him down like a bull fighter. Faced with what seemed like an immovable object, Don backed down. Pops admitted to me years later that he did diddle him. Point was, although it was mostly bluff, he had the bottle to see it through. Also Pops always made it clear, if you took the piss, there would be consequences. He didn't have to follow through on his promises many times but when he did, he never wavered, and the other party never crossed swords with him again. The only person I know who ever got away with taking the piss was me. He's never been scared of me, at least not in my warm life, and I never knew he was even capable of crying until much later on. He let me take liberties because he thought the way I was, wasn't my fault. A product of genetics on Mum's side and a bad start. He also thought he could fill the hole left by Mum with kindness. Didn't matter how I behaved, I always got what I wanted. As far as Pops was concerned whatever I did, no matter how bad, I wasn't to blame. The thing that Pops never understood was, that hole is a bottomless pit.

I gently help him back onto his feet.

"It's alright Pops. Turn off the waterworks. What would Clint Eastwood say? Let's go down to the cage."

It's a good job that Pops is handy as I don't know how we would have explained to a contractor the purpose of the cage without arousing suspicion.

I help Pops drag some boxes from the cupboard under the stairs to reveal a trap door. With a bit of limbo lean I make my way down the narrow steps of the awkward staircase, flipping the light switch as I go by. The dark cellar now emits a red glow like we are descending into hell. We're not going for dramatic effect, the red bulb was the only one left in the cupboard under the sink after the last bulb blew. Before me, there was no purpose for this space. It is cold and damp and therefore no good for people, or things which would be ruined if stored down here. It would have been a lot of work to damp proof it and Pops, although capable, never saw the point. The cellar conversion made it to the top of the list when Pops had to cage a monster. Damp proofing isn't a requirement for someone impervious to cold, containment was the main objective.

It looks like a jail cell from one of the old western films Pops loves so much. The bars are made of one inch diameter boronised steel, which in theory made them unbreakable even if a polar bear was yanking on them. Spaced six inches apart, the bars run from floor to ceiling, where they have been welded to retrofitted steel joists deep in the ground and ceiling. The door is set into the middle of the barred front and is made of the same grade of steel. Pops had done his homework in designing this.

He didn't need to use his skills for the floor and side walls as they were natural solid granite, plus, even if you got through that you were still underground. No escape from the back of the cell like the old westerns. That left the ceiling. It was out of my reach anyhow but, just in case, he'd reinforced it with solid steel plate.

I pause in the cell doorway, hand gripping each side of the entrance like I am resisting an invisible hand pushing me in. I can feel Pops' eyes on me, willing me to step forward. He sees the monochromatic image of a hunched shadow leaning against the black bars, everything else bathed in red.

"It would have been easier if you had turned a blind eye old man."

Pops, wisely, does not reply.

I let go of the entrance and walk forward the few available steps until I reach the back wall.

I hear Pops descend the last of the stairs, close the door, secure the bolt and, after a few fumbles, close the heavy-duty padlock. My resolve breaks as I launch myself at the bars. Pops topples back in surprise, banging his head on the cold stone floor. The blood which trickles down the back of his neck fills my nostrils, which mixes with the smell of fear, so that my teeth automatically elongate.

I make a noise akin to being in the middle of a hurricane, filling the tiny space as I yank at the bars, manically trying to pull them out or at least bend them enough so I can get out. Pops scrambles backwards toward the stairs, despite being well out of reach.

I feel some movement in the bars and some furniture upstairs falls over. Eventually I admit defeat though and release them.

"I'm sorry Luke," apologises Pops as he makes his way unsteadily up the steps under my intense glare.

"You will be Pops, you will be."

Sunday, 27th February, 18:52

The first stage of withdrawal should be a cause for celebration as my heartbeat returns. It's neither pleasant nor comforting (far from a baby hearing its mother's heart in her womb). It's rapid and pumps datumless fear around my body. It's like I have been drawn into a giant sowing machine and its needle is repeatedly piercing my chest at one hundred and eight stitches per minute. I know it's all in my head, a symptom of the withdrawal. My heart has been as still as stone since I transitioned from my warm life decades ago. Knowing this provides no solace as it feels as real as the life force I greedily devoured from the last nicotine dependent girl at the mouth of the alley.

You can't win with anxiety. You can have anxious thoughts which make you worry or, you can feel anxious and your mind goes in search of something to worry about.

Where's Pops? How long has it been since I last saw him? I have no idea, as by my own choice, there is no clock down here as each stroke of the second hand feels like being hit at the back of the head with a length of steel scaffolding pipe. He banged his head enough to make it bleed. He might have really hurt himself. Or I hurt him, he was running scared of me. He might have fractured his skull even. He might have bleeding on the brain. Jesus, he might be having a seizure up there!

"Pops?"

Silence.

"POPS?"

Silence.

"POPS! ARE YOU OK UP THERE?"

Silence.

"HOLD ON POPS, I'M COMING."

I give myself as much run up as possible (backed up against the cellar's far wall) and then sprint toward the cell door. I dip my shoulder at the last moment in an attempt to pop the lock. It snaps and the door swings open at high velocity, clattering against the bars, vibrating the stale air, like the tolling of a cathedral bell.

Despite my confidence in my abilities as an irresistible force, I pause in surprise that the immovable object yielded but then I remember why I busted out in the first place. I power up the steep steps, two at a time, and burst through the hatch into the hall.

Shit! It's daytime! My body clock is usually spot on. As the sun comes up, I go to sleep and then I sleep like the dead until sundown. Withdrawal wreaks havoc with these unnatural rhythms. No matter, the curtains are drawn and if I'm careful I'll be alright. I've got to find Pops.

Before I can take a step, I feel the rumble. A low frequency resonance which conducts through my feet, up my body and finally makes the tips of my ears tingle. I hear, then see, a crack develop in the far corner of the living room. It tracks down the wall from the ceiling becoming wider at the top as it traverses. The two walls which meet at the corner crunch loudly, like they are being chewed by a Rock Biter, until the outer skin ruptures and light starts to spill into the room. I watch dumbstruck as the unsupported wall can no longer stand and collapses outwards like in that Buster Keaton film. When the dust settles the wall is replaced by a solid block of azure blue. The door frame paints its own shape in brilliant sunlight, the corner of which is mere millimetres from my left foot. I instinctively jump to the side but then hear a familiar noise to my right, in the dining room.

All thoughts of Pops are forgotten as survival instinct kicks in and I grab the hatch handle to escape into the dark safety of the cellar. It doesn't budge. Maybe it's got tight as the house structure has moved. I grip the round handle with both hands, and employ my legs as well, to deadlift it open. Every muscle in my body is bulging and taught. There is no movement whatsoever. It's like I am trying to lift Thor's hammer (no surprise I ain't worthy). To my right I hear (scratch that, I feel) the heavy thud of the dining room wall collapse. A tiny corner of light kisses my foot and my eyes widen in shock of the intense pain inflicted. Pain is a good thing, pain means more adrenaline, more adrenaline means more strength as I pull even harder. I feel my shirt split across my upper back like I am turning into the Hulk. I don't really ever run out of energy (a by-product of no longer relying on oxygen to function) but I am running out of time as I hear cracks form in the wall behind me, the south facing wall. I feel the final wall fall and I have a small reprieve until the dust settles. I would like to report that my brain switched off the pain as it was so incredible (I've heard this does happen to people who experience severe injuries, dissociation I believe it is called) but I think this is a trait I left behind in my warm life. It would be more accurate to say that the pain was so intense, it was impossible to comprehend fully. What I could feel, I experienced in all its technicolour glory. On a scale of one to ten it was instantly a ten but with surprising ease found levels in excess of this, as it spread slowly from my exposed back half, across my shoulders, wrapped around my front half and finally down my arms. Before my head and eyes where enveloped, I see my arms (still gripping the hatch handle) take on the appearance of lava with bright orange emanating through cracks of greying and burnt crusts of skin. When the charring reaches my hands and fingers, I let go and join the walls on the ground. I pray (yeah me, pray!) for it to be over but it's just the beginning, as I burn with the speed of a church candle, conscious to the last glowing ember of my heart.

I open my eyes and even my foggy brain immediately recognises the steel ceiling of the cell. I am lying flat on my back on the cold, damp floor. I attempt to sit up but the safety interlocks in my brain prevent my body from obeying. I must have hurt myself. I can't feel any pain, but I give myself a moment before I try again. This time the instruction is to 'go slow' and reluctantly my body creaks into movement. My head and vision swim as I slowly reach a seated position. Once it clears, the ceiling is replaced by the shut (and clearly locked) cell door.

Pops must have snuck in a clock somewhere, as feeling returns with my head banging with a rhythmic cruelty.

On the plus side, I am not a barbeque charcoal briquette. On the downside, I am still locked up. I guess my heroic attempt resulted in me merely bouncing off the door onto my back, unmistakably banging my head hard in the process. Invulnerability to concussion is not one of my enhanced traits.

Pops is apparently OK too as there is a two litre plastic bottle of spring water pushed through the bars to my right. That wasn't there before, and there is only one man who delivers the l'eau minerale. No glass either. How uncivilised, but to be fair to the patriarch, last time he left a glass during detox, I smashed it and used the shards to remove my heart. In my delusional state, I was worried that I might accidentally fall upon the wooden chair in my cell and stake myself. The perverse logic was that if I removed my heart, and buried it in the ground, not only would it be preserved but also be safe from the chair. I lost consciousness, and collapsed, with my heart still clutched in my hand. Pops stuffed it back into the bloody cavity and then had an anxious wait to see if I woke up again. I hurt like a bitch but my chest swallowed my heart whole and I healed... eventually. Lesson learned though, no sharp or potentially sharp objects and definitely no wood.

I reach for the bottle and gasp from the pain in my right shoulder. Yep, charging the door was definitely real. Everything after that... mind playing tricks man.

I reach for the bottle again, this time with my left hand. The water inside moves like the sea as it magnifies the shakes in my hand (the only real tremor that has happened in this house today!). Despite the moving target, I manage to take a hefty chug, leaving only a dribble in the bottom. The water feels like it is still moving in my stomach as it did in the bottle. I lie back down and close my eyes, hoping the seasickness will pass.

I open my eyes and even my foggy brain immediately recognises the steel ceiling of the cell. Hang on. Haven't I been here before? I must have passed out again. A quick recap and I recall I was waiting for the seasickness to reach low tide. So far, so good. Let's try sitting up again. I said, "Let's try sitting up again." What the hell? Why can't I move?

I'm paralysed from the neck down. I lift my head to look for obvious signs of damage. It's all there: arms; legs; torso... just not doing what it's told. There is movement though, just not mine. Coils of something are efficiently moving up my body, tightening, pinning me down.

Panic summons adrenalin fuelled strength but it's already too late. The coils are too far up my arms, legs & hips. Too tight. I've no leverage to break free.

Helpless I feel one slither across my forehead and then yank my head back mercilessly, thumping it against the hard floor. That's all I need, another bang to the head!

Completely immobilised, the movement stops. What on earth is going on? Maybe, "What in earth?" is a more appropriate question as the smell of soil is unmistakeable as well as… wood? They're tree roots! This is new. I have been caught short a number of times in my cold life by daybreak, and had to bury myself, but I have never been attacked by a tree!

I can still feel the roots moving despite the fact I do not require any further securing. Their purpose becomes clear when I feel multiple needle-sharp stabs penetrate my back. The intense pain makes it impossible to cry out, as I reflex an intake of imaginary breath. I think this tree must have been a member of the Spanish Inquisition in a former life, as it understands how to push the roots deeper inside, as slowly as possible, to maximise the severity and the longevity of the pain. Despite the roots meandering course, I suspect where they are headed. However, one root loops around a rib and pulls slowly, with intent, until it snaps. I find my voice then and let out a pathetic whimper of pain. I know I have twelve pairs of ribs, and after the second and third are broken, I understand this will not be over until this arboreal monster has made twenty four wishes.

The spare rib starter finished, the roots amble toward the main course, my heart. As they reach the outer wall, they pause, clearly savouring what is to come. I recognise the behaviour based on how many times I have done it. I desperately try to wriggle free, but I am pinned as well as skewered. My escape attempt is futile and results in nothing more than new, previously undiscovered, levels of pain. How the tables have turned! The piercing of the heart muscle should be the end but it is merely another beginning of a lesson in torture. Dark blood leaks out, filling my body like a balloon before escaping at high pressure out of every orifice including my mouth, nostrils, ears and eventually my eyes (and places I don't want to specifically identify). I almost drowned when I was a kid. Pops and I were on holiday in Spain, and I fell into a swimming pool without my armbands on. He dived in and saved me, but the feeling of panic is identical. Despite my lack of reliance on oxygen I feel like I am in a perpetual state of drowning. The blood (the colour and consistency of contaminated engine oil) keeps coming and coming. I know instinctively that it's the blood of every life I have stolen being returned to the earth. This won't stop until I return every drop. Knowing this does not help with the panic, and I keep fighting to take an impossible breath against a raging torrent of ichor. After an eternity, the flow peters, and at the close, everything turns to black.

I open my eyes and even my foggy brain immediately recognises the steel ceiling of the cell. Why can't I move? Tree roots are coiling up my body, pinning me to the floor. Ah fudge nuts! I get to replay this joy again! It all happened so fast last time, I didn't get the chance to enjoy it!

The roots progression halt and I tense up in anticipation of being penetrated again. Not an exact rerun then. The tree enforcer is trying out new ways to toy with its prey.

Nothing happens for a very long time. So long in fact, I relax my body as I no longer feel threatened. I may need to give this tree some torture tuition.

"Lucas."

I know it's her even before she comes into view. Her smell, even the tone of her voice is familiar, like... mine.

"Mum?"

"Clever boy... or maybe not so clever after all. Caught by a tree?"

"I banged my head."

What the fuck Captain Birdseye! I have a had a very, very long time to think about what I would say to her and most of the words would need to be bleeped out even if this conversation was aired after the watershed. What do you think she is going to do? Whip out a bottle of Calpol and a cold compress?

She takes a few steps closer and enters my limited range of vision. Yep, definitely her. Long dark hair, green eyes, petite nose but very angular like it could cut deep. On the outside she looks beautiful. Begrudgingly I can see a lot of my most attractive features come from her. The sharply defined face and her intelligent, bewitching eyes. It must have been hard for Pops seeing her everyday looking back at him through me. She looks exactly the same as Pops' secret photo of her. Like me, she hasn't aged a day. Another thing we have in common.

She observes me like a cat eyeing a cornered mouse, a suggestion of a smile at the corners of her thin lips.

"You must have done something truly terrible to deserve treatment like this. After all, we've both done wicked things, have we not?"

I ignore the jibe. This opportunity is golden.

"Why did you leave us?"

Like a lawyer she answers a question with a question, "What reason did I have for staying?"

She's joking, I think. It's hard to tell. She's unreadable. Either way, it pushes a button.

"WHY DID YOU LEAVE, YOU FUCKING BITCH?!"

There is a long pause while she considers answering. It is clear she won't be pushed into a response by my outburst.

"Lucas, I regret with all my heart that I missed the chance to see you develop into the man you are today. You do still classify as a man, don't you? No matter. I couldn't stay. Your father made it quite clear I wasn't welcome."

"Pops? What did Pops do?"

"I remember like it was yesterday. It was a beautiful sunny day, so we were both in the garden. You were just a few weeks old, just a dot really. I'd put you in crib in the shade to keep you safe from the sun. Your father had popped home from work for some lunch. He was in a very irritable mood. I tried my best to appease him but anything I said only seemed to make him worse. He totally lost it when I said I didn't have anything to make him for lunch. I'd been too busy looking after you to go out and buy food. That's when he hit me.

I had never tasted my own blood before. It made me feel nauseous and weak. You father appeared to have grown twice the size. He was terrifying. He said I was a useless mistake, you were a mistake too and that if I didn't leave immediately on my own steam he would smash my head against every wall on the way to the front door. I scrambled along the floor, scraping my knees to ribbons, and managed to grab my purse before running out of the house. Over the sound of my heart thundering in my chest I heard him shout if I ever came back, he would snap my neck like a twig. I had no choice but to go. I was so afraid of what your father would do if I ever came back for you."

"YOU FUCKING LIAR! POPS NEVER WOULD HAVE DONE THAT!"

Her voice is quiet and steady in response to my second angry outburst.

"Suit yourself Lucas. I don't blame you. You've had years of brainwashing from your father. What did he tell you about the day I left?"

"Nothing. He won't talk about you."

"Interesting..."

"Anyway, if that story were true, then what are you doing here now?"

She answers with a knowing smile.

"Regardless, I didn't come here to reminisce."

"Then why did you come?"

"To correct a mistake."

She disappears from view and returns with a sword. It looks too heavy for her to wield but she is showing no obvious signs of effort. It has a thick, curved blade with an inscription I can't decipher,

etched into the flat of the blade. I think that type of sword is called a scimitar. It looks just like the one from that old Fry's Turkish Delight TV advert.

It's too low in here to swing the blade standing up, so she gets on her knees at a right angle to my head and shoulders. She lowers the blade slowly toward my neck to calibrate the death stroke before raising it above her head. She smiles broadly and for the first time I see her teeth.

"I should have done this while you were still inside me."

I close my eyes as the blade drops but I don't struggle.

I open my eyes and even my foggy brain immediately recognises the steel ceiling of the cell.

"Luke?"

Tak?

My mouth is so dry the words initially get stuck on the way out, "Tak?"

"No Luke, it's Pops. It's been six months. I think it's safe for you to come out now."

Monday, 31st August, 19:05

Hallucinations where I am tortured to death or Emmerdale? Tough call.

"Do you mind if I borra' vacuum cleaner Lynn? Ours has packed up."

How can Pops enjoy this endless supply of small talk drivel? He says it's been on the telly since the seventies. What kind of world do we live in where people can be entertained by the constant repetition of, "Goin' t' Woolpack?" and "Where's *fill in the blank with name*?", "He's on top field." If there was a button on the TV remote to drop another plane on that cursed village, I'd keep my finger permanently on it. Albert Square and Coronation Street too. Emmerdale is just a turd flavoured starter with two more courses to follow!

Apart from being Pops' comfort blanket, the soaps do offer some fringe benefits. A knowledge of the soaps can be as useful as a lighter in my hunting toolkit. However, I am abstaining, so I have no use for them at present.

"Want anything from the shops, Pops?"

Nothing. That TV is better at mind manipulation than I am.

"YO POPS, SHOPS!"

"What?"

"Shops, Pops. Do you want any cakes, Flakes, mags, fags, chips, dips, chains…"

"I'm good Luke."

His eyes return to the screen and glaze over.

Mon dieu! It's bright in here but wearing sunglasses at night in November may draw attention.

I am not one hundred percent sure why I even go to the Co-op. I don't eat. I need to drink fluids, otherwise I dehydrate and get all crispy. There's no point buying more bottled water as there is enough in the dining room to put out a house fire. I don't really drink alcohol at home. That's more of a cover when I go out hunting. Rewind the tape and you will be reminded that drugs do have an effect on me and, although the effect is negligible, the habit of drinking coffee has followed me into my cold life. Again, we have jars of instant BOGOF coffee 3 layers deep in the kitchen cupboard.

I linger by the magazines and my eyes are drawn to the bare necks & shoulders of the semi clad ladies on the top shelf. Something stirs inside me. I feel like a penniless beggar staring up at the menu in McDonalds.

"Not as good as the real thing."

"What the shit! Where did you appear from? Did you spring up out of the floor?"

"You were engrossed. I could have been an approaching avalanche and I don't think you would have noticed until you were half buried. As a matter of interest, are you looking at the naked women or the men?"

I had been ambushed into this conversation and without consideration of whether I wanted to continue, I get swept up in its momentum.

"The women. I like the look of the bottles more."

She giggles which in turn makes me smile. She wanders off leaving me to wonder what just happened. The grey apron gives her away as staff although I don't recall ever seeing her before.

"I know I'm a couple of quid short but just give me the fucking bottle and stop acting like you give a shit."

Uh-oh, trouble in paradise. What's this all about?

I peer round the queue to get a better view of the drama enfolding at the front. Who needs Eastenders? It's all happening at the Co-op!

The Coca-Cola girl from the magazine aisle is manning the till now and clearly needing to draw upon all of her customer service training.

"There's an ATM over there sir. You can get some money from there."

"I ain't got a bank card with me and I ain't leaving without that bottle of whiskey. So, stop being a cunt and hand it over."

Whoa! He dropped the C-Bomb! God's doing the washing up somewhere and has now dropped a soapy glass in shock.

I look back expecting to see another member of staff coming to her aid. She's either working this shift alone or there is some pimply, seventeen year old pretending this is not happening, busying himself in the stock room. No-one in the queue seems keen to get involved either. Ballons! Why do I have to play the hero? It's the one thing that I am definitely not.

It takes me a surprisingly long time to get to the front of the line. Initially people seem to think that I am just trying to get a better view, or jump the queue, so they are reluctant to move. Once they get the idea that I am on my way to sort this out, they can't get out of the way quick enough.

"Listen carefully you cunt..."

He did it again! In heaven God drops a plate covered in suds or is that thunder?

"Want some help?"

Her brow crinkles as she looks at me quizzically.

Her mouth betrays a slight smile as she says, "Well, you could open another till. There is quite a long queue forming." This time she upgrades my previous smile to a laugh out loud.

"Not what I had in mind."

"Are you going to lend him the rest of the money then?"

Again, the faintest hint of a smile escapes and forms on her lips.

Clearly feeling left out of the conversation Mr. R. Sole acknowledges my presence as he glances back to his left to address me formally.

"Fuck off mate. Wait your fucking turn, there's a good boy."

He's clearly not threatened by me as he refocusses his entire attention on the Coca-Cola girl. He looks about three times my weight. From the smell of him (taking my enhanced senses out of the equation) I reckon if I licked his bull neck, he would taste of pure alcohol. Maybe I should I give it go. On second thoughts he does seem a bit grouchy.

I hit him hard and fast in the back of the head mid-way through his third C-Bomb. He stumbles forwards hitting his head on the plexiglass separating him from the Coca-Cola girl. She involuntarily calls out, evidently, I took her by surprise too. He bounces back like I've got him on an invisible bungy cord. I catch him by the scruff of his jacket before he falls down unconscious.

I shake him up and down, so his head wobbles back and forth, giving the impression that his mouth is opening and closing.

I do my best to not move my lips (ventriloquism is not one of my talents) when I say, "I am very sorry I bothered you miss. I've had a bit too much to drink. I'm going to go and have a sleep in that skip now."

The Coca-Cola girl claps a hand over her mouth to stifle a loud laugh which erupts.

I drag secret shopper (well he might be, like a method actor mystery shopper) outside accompanied by a round of applause from the other customers in the queue. True to his word he goes for a little nap in a skip across the road with a little help from me to tuck him in.

I don't return to retrieve my shopping.

That girl shone like the sun.

Thursday, 3rd September, 21:29

"Luke."

"Yeah Pops?"

"Can you pass me a toilet roll. There's none in here."

"Oh come on Pops! You must have known there was none before you started. You are the only one in the house who uses it!"

"What can I say, it's my age. I forget things. Just pass me one around the door."

"What do you mean your age? I used to have to do this when I was a kid. It was bad enough then and that was before I had an enhanced sense of smell!"

Despite my reservations I pass him a roll through the gap in the door.

"Jesus Pops! You didn't even put the fan on!"

Never mind eau de garlic. If this brown cloud was condensed into a perfume, then no woman would ever need to worry about me biting them ever again. I quickly retreat to a safe distance and consider a change of clothes, or at least a walk to air them. I think we have now established the true source of evil in this family lives inside of Pops.

There is a merciful flush and then Pops makes his way down the stairs.

"I swear you did that on purpose."

"As if I would," he replies, but I see a suggestion of a smirk as he passes me on his way to the kitchen.

"Coffee Luke?"

"No thanks Pops."

"Do you remember that time in B&Q?"

"What do you mean 'that time in B&Q'? We were there more times than we went to the playground. It was like getting parole when Tak came to live with us so I didn't have to go with you."

"You exaggerate Luke."

Every week, sometimes twice a week, I swear to God. While other kids went to soft play, I went to look at paint. It's no wonder I used to wander off to find some fun.

"Ahhh. Now I know what you are talking about. That was a clear-cut case of neglect. I should have called Childline!"

I can hear him chuckling to himself in the kitchen and, despite myself, I can't help smiling too.

I don't think I can do this story justice. I think Pops will do a better job than me. I wouldn't usually dip into his thoughts (feels disrespectful somehow) but I'm sure he wouldn't mind for this. Plus, it will show it was one hundred percent his fault!

"Where are we going Dad?"

"Soft play."

"Really?"

"No, just kidding, I've got to pop into B&Q for something."

Luke folds his arms tightly across his chest and his forehead pinches into a scowl. I shouldn't tease him, but he looks so cute when he's having a strop.

"How about I get you a Mars Bar from the vending machine on the way out?"

His brow releases for a moment. The offer of a Mars Bar is tempting. It's not enough of a bribe though, as he screws up his face again and stares over the dashboard without answering. I up the ante.

"And a can of coke?"

That did the trick.

He could let go of my hand (we're in the store now not the car park) but he holds on with his soft hands, gripping on to two of my fingers.

"Dad?"

"Yeah?"

"I need the toilet."

"What!? I told you to go before we left the house."

Unbelievable! How many times do we have to have this conversation?

"I know Dad, but I didn't need to go then."

"Can you hold it?"

"Yes Dad."

"Good boy. We won't be long."

Paint? Paint? Paint? Here we are, aisle 4. Now where is that test card. I search my jeans pockets but come up empty. What the hell? I specifically remember putting it in my back pocket this morning so I wouldn't forget it. But that was before... before Luke knocked his Vimto all over me at lunch and soaked them. He did a proper job. I even had to change my underpants. Note to self not to let him sit on my lap whilst eating his lunch. The cascade of the crimson fluid made it look like he had opened a vein in my neck!

No point going home for it, as mistake number two was putting said jeans straight into the washing machine before we left. When I get back the test card will have disintegrated, and all the clothes will now be covered in tiny pieces of cardboard!

A green sea of matt emulsion lies ahead of me, but which one was it? There is every shade from 'white that has been walked through a room where they make green paint' all the way to 'Nordic forest in the middle of a cloudy night during winter solstice'. I close my eyes and try to recall the name of the shade. I can recreate the colour card in my head. I know the position on the card it was at, and I can see the name masked with an asterisk but the writing is blurred, like I haven't got my glasses on. 'Beefy Blow'? No, that can't be right. Maybe Luke will remember. He helped me pick the colour.

I look down to my left, where Luke had been holding my hand moments before. Luke? Not there. My stomach drops a couple of floors. On the small chance I am mistaken, I look to my right.

Luke? My stomach drops another couple of floors. My head whips back and forth, looking in both directions down the paint aisle. No sign of him. Shit! Cue my stomach going into freefall.

Keep calm! Keep calm! I resist the urge to run and walk (albeit double time) back to the central aisle. I make my way back toward the exit, pausing at each intersection to look left and right down the aisles. The store is thankfully quiet, so I get clear views. I reach the exit empty handed and have a decision to make. Search the car park or double back and check the aisles at the rear of the shop. If someone has taken him, I will have a chance to intercept the bastard in the car park. I take a step toward the open air before I check myself. That's the panic talking. He's likely just one aisle up from the paint. I just went the wrong way. I can no longer resist the pull of the adrenaline and I jog up and past where we were. Despite my single-minded focus, it's impossible to ignore the smell of the drains at this end of the store. Whoa, that stinks!

"Dad!"

Luke? I follow the source of the call and spot the little angel's head peering from around a partition.

My body is still pumped full of adrenaline, which seems to be working its way up from my legs to my mouth, where a few choice words (likely inappropriate for little ears) are about to form on my lips.

"Dad!"

"You scared me half to death you little..."

Jesus Christ! The smell is so bad my eyes struggle to stay open for fear they will let in more of the pong.

I round the partition, and despite my better judgement, my mouth drops open.

"Dad, have you got any toilet paper? There's none here."

Luke's pants and trousers are dangling, hooked on his feet which don't reach the floor yet. He is sat forward, literally on the porcelain of a toilet in a showroom bathroom. Despite many conversations on this subject Luke still doesn't get the idea of using the seat!.

Completely disarmed I answer his question.

"No, I haven't got anything like that on me."

I regain my composure a little, despite the smell which is beginning to make my ears ring!

"Pull your trousers up Luke."

As he dismounts, I peer behind him into the bowl. Jesus lord! It's like a Damien Hirst! A perfectly laid and crimped turd (glistening under the intense strip lights) in a pristinely, white toilet bowl. Despite the unbreathable atmosphere, I can't stop staring at it. It's bigger than I could manage! Even a working flush wouldn't be capable of despatching that!

"Dad? These taps don't work."

Snapped out of my poo trance I look over at Luke at the equally unplumbed basin.

"We need to go Luke."

"But I haven't washed my hands. You told me I've always got to wash my hands after using the toilet. Especially after a number two."

"You can do it when we get home."

"What about the vending machine Dad. You promised."

"OK, OK, but we are going to have to be quick."

Out in the blessedly uncontaminated air outside I mutter under my breath, "Won't be able to go back to that B&Q again."

"What did you say Dad?" *enquires Luke, proudly brandishing his Mars Bar and coke.*

"Nothing son."

It's not until we make good on our escape to the bypass do I start to chuckle softly.

"What's funny Dad?"

"Nothing really, just a funny thought."

Saturday, 5th September, 22:11

I love bus shelters. You can feel alive in a bus shelter. The wind and rain whip right through its unsided design and your face becomes a satellite dish for picking up Mother Earth's signal, all without getting soaking wet. Tonight, is no different, and a gust of wind peppers my face with rain which must only be a degree above hale. I have my fingers crossed for a storm, but I can't feel the low thrum of electricity where the back of my head meets my neck (a.k.a. the 'heck') which precedes the anger of Thor.

Maybe the Thunder God has visited here lately as it looks like he has blasted a hole through the back of the shelter, with lightning sent forth from Mjölnir. More likely it was 'Fish Finger' using a lighter. He has signed his work in lurid green spray paint. Oh wait, there's more, "Lisa... sucks... cock!" Well, it's good to keep abreast of local news. Maybe I am looking at this all wrong. Maybe this whole bus shelter is a piece of modern art. Maybe 'Fish Finger' is the new Banksy? If he is, I still don't get it.

Enough culture and I settle down on the folded down plastic seat, close my eyes and focus on the sound of the wind and the sensation of the mild sting of the rain. I bet you are wondering what I do if a bus stops? For one thing, buses are more of a daytime thing, so no chance of me being out unless someone invents SPF 10,000 sun cream. The night buses that do come along may slow down but generally speed up when the driver spies that I appear to be sparked out. Some are kind enough to stop to give me the opportunity of climbing aboard. As long as I keep up the pretence, they drive off pretty soon afterwards. No-one ever risks getting out to check on me. If anyone ever thought about it, I would push the thought straight out of their heads. Some, I swear, speed up when they see a person at the bus stop and all you know about it is when you feel the rush of air as it passes. No buses tonight yet, just the wind whistling through.

"They drive straight past unless you keep an eye out and wave them down."

I do the impossible and manage to jump while seated. The seat springs back and pinches my arse as gravity halts my ascent.

"Holy chlorinated chicken balls!" I exclaim, "The Co-op job must be a cover, you have the ninja skills of a top dollar assassin!"

It's next to impossible to sneak up on someone with superhuman senses like mine. She's managed it twice!

"You're pretty jittery for someone who takes on dudes twice his size."

Again, I detect the slightest hint of a smile on the Coca-Cola Girl's lips as she takes a seat.

"Why don't you sit down?" I ask as if she is still standing and like it's my bus shelter.

"Don't mind if I do."

No doubt about it, that smile makes another appearance.

I close my eyes again, hoping this will deter her from continuing the second conversation she has ambushed me into. It does little to block out her bright light.

"I'll wake you when the bus gets here. It's the least I can do, you know, after what you did. I saw him get out of the skip you know. He looked very confused. There was a banana skin on his head. It looked like a designer hat! Someone must have thrown it away in the skip. I mean, you wouldn't expect anyone to be in there, would you?"

The mental image of that useless lump of meat extricating himself from the skip with a banana hat is clear and very funny. Despite myself I smirk and then curse inwardly. I bet she saw that.

"Anyway, what I am trying to say is, thanks and I'll promise I'll wake you up."

"Don't bother," I answer without opening my eyes, "I'm not getting on."

"What do you mean, 'you're not getting on?' It's the last bus!"

"I'm taking in the night."

"From under a bus shelter?"

"I don't like getting wet."

I hear the laugh which escapes her.

"I'm Dani, by the way."

"L...," I try to resist telling her my name, like I am trying very hard to kill this conversation. I've still got my eyes closed for Christ's sake!, "Lucas."

"Is this your favourite bus stop? I mean, do you come here often?"

Is she trying to pick me up? I have to put a stop to this.

"Look. I know what I look like on the outside but I'm not really a man. Well, I haven't been for quite some time now and I don't think you'd like where this would go."

"Wow."

"Shocking huh?"

"No, I mean wow. Well seeing as this is confession time, I may as well come clean too. You know things in nature can start off as one thing and then can transform into something else? Like a nymph changing into a Dragonfly?"

What is with this girl? I was being uncharacteristically honest to put her off and bring this conversation to an abrupt halt. Instead of that we have ended up sharing something personal about ourselves, achieving the opposite, she got my attention.

I open my eyes to look at her and reply, "What?"

A shout from across the road kills the conversation better than I, evidently, could.

"Oi! Freak! What the fuck do you think you are doing in my bus shelter?"

"Oh shit!" she murmurs.

In comparison to her handling of the secret shopper, this time I can sense her fear. It's not good for someone like me to pick up on that. My eyes are drawn back to the graffiti. I manage to catch her eye despite the fact she is looking at the ground trying her best to look small and invisible.

"Fish Finger?" I ask gently.

She lowers her head slightly but it's hard to tell as she is shaking. I glance over at the apparent owner of this bus shelter. He has the face of someone in their late teens / early twenties, just a kid really. He is advancing menacingly across the road towards us, followed by three lackeys. I look back at the Coca-Cola Girl trying to assess her age.

"Old school friend?"

Another shaky nod.

Sadly, the bus is too late to marmalise him on the way over. That would have brought this scene to an a sudden but highly amusing end.

"I said, 'what the fuck do you think...'"

Up until this point he has only had eyes for her. His scowl evaporates, and changes into a stupid look of surprise, when I stand and block his path.

I am instantly inside his personal space, and he stops like he has just bumped into a patio door.

"Fish? Or do you prefer Mr. Finger?"

"What?"

"Are you a direct descendant of Captain Birdseye? You don't have the family beard. Maybe related by marriage?"

"What?"

"Ohh! Fish Finger! I get it now. You are such a catch that women practically throw themselves at you to have the honour of being finger banged by such a renowned stud. Add to that, a lack of personal hygiene. Then bingo! A name any man would be proud to emblazon onto a bus shelter. Can I give you a bit of advice mate? If I'm right about the quality of girls a man like you would attract, I wouldn't recommend picking your nose afterwards."

I hear a stifled laugh behind me. That's encouraging. Unfortunately, he hears it too and it snaps him out of his surprise.

"Do you think she'll let you fuck her if you act the big man? I'm almost tempted to let it slide so you can find out the truth for yourself."

We are like two boxers at an ill-tempered weigh in. I raise my eyebrows a bit to make my eyes widen. I want him in no doubt that I'm staring him down. We are about the same height and build. In normal circumstances I think it would be a fair fight. As much fun as it would be to see this bully scuttle away with his tail between his legs, I am secretly glad he has found his bottle. This bus shelter is clearly his tiny kingdom, plus he has three amigos to back him up. If I can't feed, I'll take graphic violence as Canderel.

I'm surprised when the Coca-Cola Girl gently puts her hand on my arm and deescalates the situation, which is moments away from igniting.

"Please. Not for me."

Her touch draws all the aggression out of me and I disengage. Maybe I'm not the only one with superpowers.

"OK Dani, I'll walk you home instead."

I am listening for it, but they don't give chase.

Still within hearing distance I hear Fish Finger shout, "You'd better watch your back man. I is gonna make you bleed out."

Oh, that's scary! What could he possibly do to me?

Saturday, 12th September, 02:54

You don't buy enough loo roll to stretch to the moon shopping in the Co-op. Especially if you are a bargain hunter of the prowess of Pops, who would prefer to 'no wipe' for a week than pay a few extra pence per roll. No, for that type of bulk buy bargain, you have to go to one of those giant supermarkets. One of those where you can buy a multitude of different brands of baked beans in tomato sauce but never find all the ingredients to make a meal from scratch (trust me, I have tried many times for Father's Day). As well as being able to procure enough toilet roll that you may need to bequeath it to your next of kin, these food warehouses have another advantage. Apart from God's Day, they are open 24 hours which means I can tag along and do the heavy lifting without fear I will get chargrilled.

We are in the beans aisle, and I am still staggered by the 'Berlin Wall of Beans' which, I wager, no-one could tell apart in a blind taste test. I couldn't tell the difference and I have a superhuman sense of smell! No-one in the world except for Pops, who claims he could taste one rogue bean in a bath of Heinz. Tonight, is Heinz Baked Beans day, which means it's 2 for 1. Pops drops down to grab a full, film covered tray like a starving man chasing a rolling chicken nugget. He heaves like a strongman attempting a new deadlift personal best, but the beans don't even clear his knees.

"You alright Pops?"

He straightens up slowly still eyeballing the tray, contemplating a second attempt.

"Just getting old Luke. Let me catch my breath and I'll try again."

I know he is no spring chicken, but this weight would not ordinarily cause him any issues.

"It's alright Pops. Let me do it. It's what I'm here for."

I hook my little finger underneath the thick, plastic overpacking and deftly place the tray in the trolley and push on.

"I want two more trays."

"You serious Pops?"

How many tins of beans can one man eat?

"They'd better not refuse us at the till," I warn.

I flip in a couple more trays and we move on.

My fun via a trolley slide comes to an abrupt halt when I see what Pops is up to. We're in the bread aisle now, so almost done. Despite the fact I should have gotten used to this by now, I am wishing myself to be anywhere but here. It looks like the bottom shelf has thrown up half a dozen loaves of bread so it can swallow Pops. All you can see is a pair of grubby jeans and shoes (fit for the clothes recycling) sticking out into the aisle. His legs scramble back and forth as the maw coughs up another loaf.

"A-ha! Got it!" he proclaims, like he has drawn the sword from the stone, as he tries ungracefully to extricate himself from the shelf.

Although I want this to be over and then disassociate this memory (file it away under 'DO NOT OPEN' until we next go food shopping) I resist the temptation of getting involved and pulling him out. There is a small chance that someone passing may not assume we are together. Eventually he gets to his feet and holds aloft the loaf of bread by its tied end like it was a 30 lb river trout.

"Worth it Pops?"

"Yep. Much better date."

"By how much?"

"A day."

"A day?!"

My incredulousness does nothing to take the shine off his win. It's like he's scored the winning goal at the FA Cup.

"You picking up that mess Pops?" I say, inclining my head to the multiple loaves of bread littering the polished floor.

Massaging the small of his back with his hand Pops replies, "No, are you?"

"No."

"Well let's roll then," says Pops, clearly still buzzing, "See what I did then? You're pushing a trolley. A trolley's got wheels, wheels that..."

"I get it Pops. It's just not funny."

But if that woman is still on shift, that I spied when we came in, then this trip won't be a dead loss.

It's the last stop before the tills, the mineral water aisle. For the first time tonight, we share the space with some post party clubbers, clearly on the search for some liquid refreshment. My eyes are instantly drawn to the exposed necks of the two girls in the group, dressed in vest tops and short skirts. Whatever they have put into their system tonight is still keeping their heart rates high and I can hear the strong pulses in their necks calling out to me. I could be drinking that bliss, feeling the blood pumping through me, and experiencing that moment of euphoria when you feel their last heart beats as your own. It's only when Pops grabs my arm do I notice he is calling my name.

"Luke?"

I can hear the fear in his voice.

"Are you there son?"

With my voice sounding far away, I reply, "Yeah Pops. I'm back."

We walk past the group, but it feels like I am dragging heavy weights chained to my ankles. The girls look up as I pass because I can't stop my mind calling out to them. It would be so easy to get them to wait outside for me. It wouldn't take long to reach a place out of view of the CCTV. The camera wouldn't detect me anyway, so it would just look like they wandered off together. With a monumental effort I break the connection. Newly formed sweat on my brow makes me feel cold and I think I've bent the handle of the trolley. It's definitely not steering right now.

No.

No.

No.

Yes. As I suspected, she's perfect. The cashier has a friendly face, looks chatty and (most importantly) she's slightly chubby. When she sees me approaching, she smiles warmly but when she sees Pops her eyes practically light up.

I am not 100% sure what he's got, but there is a certain demographic of heterosexual women that can't get enough of Pops. My hypothesis is that it's the dishevelled look that he rocks: messy hair; wrinkled clothes. He's like a real life Columbo. He's even got the beat-up car. Basically he looks like he needs looking after and he seems to have a plentiful supply of women offering to do it. But for some reason I can't fathom, they are all slightly overweight too.

I throw all our stuff onto the conveyor and push the trolley to the other end, ready to load up again. I don't need to dip into her thoughts to see what she is thinking.

As she scans the beans she says, "I'm not really supposed to sell them like this, but you seem very nice so I'm happy to turn a blind eye."

Even though he is embarrassed, he plays along. Man, is there nothing Pops won't do for cheap beans? It's a big shop, so he is going to have to keep this up for a long time. Minutes later (I reckon for Pops if felt more like hours) she hands him back his change and the receipt. She's written something on it. She said it was a discount code, but the first 5 digits are the same as our phone area code and the last digit is an 'X'. She takes the opportunity to give his hand an affectionate squeeze and I snort a laugh, which I convincingly cover up as a sneeze. The 'sneeze' reminds her that I am there, and she says, "Bless you." before returning her attention back to Pops.

"It's kind of your Grandson to help you. You'd think he'd be out partying. Maybe see you soon sweetheart. I'm always on the graveyard shift Wednesdays."

I'm still chuckling to myself as I get in the passenger seat of the Columbomobile.

Eyeing me with narrow eyes, Pops starts the conversation, "You picked her on purpose, didn't you?"

"Yep. Her till had the shortest queue."

"It's 4am Luke! There aren't any queues!"

There's a pause and somewhere a penny, or maybe a loaf of bread, drops.

"You were getting your own back for the bread aisle, weren't you?"

"She looked... comfy. Plus, she looked the other way to your 'planning for the zombie apocalypse' buying."

"We won't be able to come here on a Wednesday again!"

We drive in silence for a few minutes.

"Pops, what's in the locked box?"

"Huh?"

"When you tried to lift the tray of beans, this locked box appeared in your mind. You know I do my best not to skim your thoughts, but you were practically broadcasting it."

"I don't know what you are talking about Luke."

"Ah come on Pops. You know, the one that has a picture of a cowboy on it."

There's a sharpness to his response, that he tries unsuccessfully to hide, when he replies, "Like I said, 'I don't know what you are talking about.' But whatever it is, if it's in a locked box then that must mean it's none of your business."

I drop the subject and resist the temptation to dip into his thoughts and pry it open. The memory of when I last opened a box without permission is still vividly fresh.

Wednesday, 16th September, 18:59

Donald J. Trump! How bright does it need to be? People come here to talk, not perform open heart surgery! The good thing about living in a large city is that you can easily switch to a new A.A. group when you leave a bit of mess at the last one. There is comfort in the familiarity of the set up but if there was one thing I would change, it would be the lighting which is always one lumen shy of looking directly at the sun. I decide to keep my eyes shut until the kick off. People will just assume I am asleep after pulling an all nighter.

I hear a scrape as the meeting chair arrives and starts to go through the standard preliminaries. I open my eyes as slowly as possible to give them the maximum amount of time to acclimatise. The scene is as expected, with never a more morose group gathered together since the last Morrissey farewell gig. All human embodiments of black holes whose gravity is attuned to suck in all the fun and joy out of life. All except the bright spark plug sat to my right, who has the uncanny ability to reappear out of a trapdoor that evidently tracks me as reliably as my shadow.

"Did you follow me here?" we both whisper, which has the effect of doubling the volume and incurring a sharp look from the A.A. Group Leader who has yet to finish his opening spiel.

"Seriously, I will be afraid to blink soon!" I exclaim.

I am half serious but the laugh which Dani manages to stifle makes it clear she finds the comment endearing.

In a hushed tone, I ask a stupid question, "What are you doing here?"

Which is answered in a deserving manner, "What do you think I am doing here? I'm here for the free drinks."

She looks straight ahead as she speaks to give the impression she is paying attention to the group leader but I can see she wants to laugh at her own joke. I don't blame her. It's good enough to raise the corners of my mouth.

Our 'Captain Morgan' raises his voice to make a point fired in our direction, "I can see we have some new members tonight. It's a nice surprise to have a couple join us. The couple that struggles together, stays together, eh?"

Couple?

Dani hides a giggle using my trademark move of pretending to sneeze.

She leans in close to my ear, still covering her mouth so as not to suffer the wrath of our dear Captain, and whispers, "Actually, I come for the tales of woe."

Whoa! I have a déjà vu shiver like she was able to delve into my thoughts.

I've got to be honest, I didn't hold out much hope for Clive. But when his verbal meanderings arrived at, "...I didn't really see the harm in premium rate numbers, even though they did tip me into a little bit of debt..." my thoughts proclaimed Bingo!

"Bingo!" Dani's whisper echoes my inner voice.

If she keeps doing that I will stop being surprised soon.

"It had become a bit of a routine. I'd get hammered, then I would call one of those premium rate numbers and flog myself until my old boy was as red as Darth Vader's light sabre. That was the trouble of phoning these numbers well and truly blottoed. It was like being injected with a local anaesthetic. It also turned what should have been a £5 Hand Solo into a £50 wankathon.

I'd been out with my fiancé earlier in the evening. She'd moved on to meet some friends, but you know what it's like, you can't have just a couple. Anyway, fast forward about ten pints and I am back at my flat. It's about 2 a.m. and I've got my boxers round my ankles, tissues and baby oil at the ready, phone on speaker and speed dialling my favourite premium rate number. The familiar female voice at the other end of the line sounds a bit groggy when she asks me what I want, but in my inebriated state I just assume I'm her last call at the end of a long shift. Anyway, I proceed to tell her what I want, which is, that she describes herself dressed as an Austrian milk maid with long white socks, short skirt and a top so low-cut that her large chest is in serious danger of falling out. Next, she will direct me to get on all fours while she gives me the 'milking' of my life until I do my best to fill a strategically placed metal bucket. Once done she will drink my produce before proclaiming, 'Hmmm! Devon knows how they make it so creamy!' Having finished detailing my list of requirements, the voice at the other end of the phone replies (ever more so alert now), 'Clive? Is that you?' My Clive Anderson instantly shrinks to the size of an acorn hitching a ride on two walnuts. The familiar voice isn't my 'usual' recognising one of her regulars, rather my soon to be Mother-in-Law. My fiancé (Becca) had joked before that, 'wouldn't it be funny if we ever got our phones mixed up?' We had exactly the same make and model with the key difference that her number one speed dial was not the 'Busty Euro Babes' premium rate number. I panicked, pretended I had rung the wrong number and hung up. But there was no getting out of it. Both Becca and her Mum knew exactly who 'Betsy' the cow was. Becca and I have never even had phone sex so she it took it very personally, as if I'd been cheating on her. She broke off the engagement leaving me to cover ten thousand pounds of non-refundable wedding expenses. Add to that the credit card debt from the excessive drinking and extravagant wanking. That's when I finally admitted to myself that I had a problem."

A pack of hyenas must have escaped from the zoo and snuck into the hall behind us, as there erupted a cacophony of devilish cackling. Oh no, my mistake. That was just the echo from mine & Dani's howls when we reached a point where we couldn't hold it in anymore. The A.A. Leader majestically rises to his feet and points towards the exit. Holding our sides in, doubled over like we are escaping heavy enemy gunfire, we stumble towards the door. It feels like the giggles will never cease as the memory of Clive's 'Tale of the Pail' keeps reigniting them but eventually the laughing (and crying) dries up.

"Pub?" I propose.

Where else would two people go after an A.A. meeting?

Thursday, 1st October, 21:01

I must be in an uncharacteristically good mood, because I let Pops talk me into watching a war movie on the telly. It's got that look that only old movies have, like they used a different colour palette to more modern films. It's the 'Dirty Dozen' and I must admit that this is the first time I have actually sat down and watched this from the start. If this had been on at any other time, and Pops was watching, I would have found something else to do. The story is about a bunch of murderers who are given a second chance to be good guys. Is Pops playing Goebbels and trying to send me some sort of subliminal message?

Despite myself, I'm enjoying the movie history lesson. It's the father, possibly grandfather, of 'Suicide Squad'. I can't stand films where the main character hasn't got any flaws. The Dirty 'Baker's' Dozen, even if you include Reisman, have enough flaws between them to build a skyscraper! How can anyone empathise with a Mr. Perfect? I guess the film-makers recognised that when they made Superman 3, but man, that film sucked balls. I can see why Pops likes the Dirty Dozen too. He would have been in his early twenties when this film came out. He was a post-war child so who better to be the baddies than the Nazis, and the perfect weapon? Monsters of our own. Plus, I reckon Pops fancies himself as Marvin's character. Someone who never takes a backward step, tells it straight and is a believer in the ends justifying the means. This is a broader history lesson than I first thought. Pops learnt it from Marvin and I learnt it from Pops.

"Yo Pops. Is anyone in this film still alive? Or should this film be retitled to the 'Dead' Dozen?"

"I think Donald Sutherland is still alive and the black fella. I think he was an American Football player or something. The film won an Oscar, I think. Oh, and that big guy was on Bonanza."

"Don't get any ideas Pops. I'll do a war movie but I ain't following that up with a side order of Bonanza."

An ad break comes on and I yawn, stretching out both arms. I look over at Pops on the other sofa who does likewise.

"Coffee Pops?"

"Yes, please Luke."

I wander to the kitchen and whack the kettle on, grab a couple of stained mugs and add a generous teaspoon of instant coffee to both. Even over the sound of the kettle, I hear the TV go quiet for about 30 seconds or so. I return to the living room and put our steaming mugs on the coffee table. Coffee table! I just got that!

"Thanks Luke."

"Something up with the TV Pops?"

"What?"

"The TV. It went quiet for a bit."

Pops broadcasts that box with the cowboy on it again. The image is fuzzy so I can't tell if it's the same face as the guy from Bonanza. I do notice that he has a red shirt on this time.

The film starts up again, and I get the distinct impression that Pops feels like he has been saved by the bell.

The 'volunteers' have just finished their training when the second ad break starts. There are a surprising number of commercial breaks for such an old film. I am maxed out on caffeine so don't offer again and I am not surprised Pops doesn't offer to return the favour. The ads are appropriate for the expected audience (I'm not counting myself here), ads for walk in baths and Stannah stair lifts. The joys of getting old, eh? An ad comes on for Macmillan and the box in Pops' mind returns and grows to about four metres high and eight metres across. The cowboy in the hat has grown to gigantic proportions. It's not the bloke from 'Bonanza' it's…

"Who the hell is the Marlboro Man?"

Pops looks stricken and doesn't reply. The edges of the box are starting to leak a black viscous, tar like substance. The front and sides are beginning to bulge outwards, presumably backing up more of this foul liquid that smells like a cremation smoothie. The front of the box bursts open on its hinges but, instead of more tar, colossal cigarettes (about three and a half metres tall) start tumbling out. An impossible number flow out, much more than the box could possibly contain. I snap back to my optical eyes and on the TV see a nurse talking to a skeleton with skin with a drip in his arm. I look back at Pops. If he could read my mind, I am sure he would see a penny, the size of a monster truck tyre, dropping to the ground causing trees to fall as it lands. I jump straight in at DEFCON 3.

"YOU GOT FUCKING CANCER AGAIN?!" I spit.

Pops doesn't need to answer to confirm it. You don't even need to be a mind reader to tell. His face says it all. I do my best to keep a lid on my bubbling anger, less I move to DEFCON 2.

Through gritted teeth, I try to keep the venom out of my voice, "How long have you known?"

He's looking down at the TV remote and is rubbing his thumb back and forth across one of the rubber keys. He eventually finds his voice which is quiet.

Addressing the remote control he says, "It was during your last relapse."

Gentlemen, we are now at DEFCON 2, next step global thermonuclear war. FUCKING HELL! THAT'S NEARLY A YEAR AGO! I want to scream this in his face but manage to keep it as an internal monologue. Pops does look at me now but looks away quickly as if there is an autocue running on my forehead, detailing my inner thoughts. I am equally sure of this as much as he knows what my next question will be.

"How bad is it?"

"Pretty bleak. The doctors have stopped giving me predictions now. I am in unknown territory."

"So the treatment didn't work? What did you have? An op? Radiotherapy? Chemotherapy?"

"I didn't go for any treatment, Luke."

Gentlemen, we are now at DEFCON 1, nuclear war imminent.

"WHAT THE FUCK DO YOU MEAN, 'YOU DIDN'T HAVE ANY TREATMENT?', YOU SELFISH, OLD BASTARD? YOU CAN'T LEAVE ME ON MY OWN!"

The silence that follows is somehow louder than my last outburst. It's probably just as well that Pops breaks it.

"Luke, I was scared. People my age go into hospital and don't come back out again. Maybe if someone could have gone in with me, it would have been a different story."

"Don't you bloody blame me for this!"

"No, Luke, that's not what I meant. I'm tired. It was almost a relief to know I wouldn't have to be tired anymore. You don't look a day over 20 and you have looked that way for decades. I don't even know if you can die of old age. You were always going to outlive me. You must have known that."

Oh yes, I knew that, just buried it deep with all the other thoughts I don't want to face. Like the screams of countless, dead girls begging to be spared. My head is spinning like a set of index cards attached to a motor. There has got to be a way out of this shit show. I manage to jam the motor and a card becomes visible. They say the best ideas are simple and usually staring you in the face.

"I'll turn you."

"What?"

"I'll turn you Pops. Make you like me. You'll be immortalised as a silver haired hobo, but that's never posed you any particular issue in attracting the opposite sex. Well, the plus sizes anyway."

"No. Besides, you don't even know how you came to be, let alone how to do it."

"I'll Google it."

"No," says Pops with a Marvin like unwavering firmness.

"What if I don't give you a choice?"

"I don't think even you would do that."

Pops' thoughts reveal that he is not one hundred percent sure of that.

"I'm so tired Luke. I can't do this anymore. I just want some peace."

My brain is misfiring all over the place, making it near impossible to piece together a train of thought. I manage to thread the following together: he's dying (almost dead actually); he won't help himself; he's going to leave me on my own and he doesn't give a shit! If there is a DEFCON 0, I have reached it and I turn into the mushroom cloud. I rise quickly to my feet and begin to rain verbal abuse down upon his vulnerable form.

"REST IN PIECE EH? I SEE TO IT YOU REST IN PIECES YOU DECREPID OLD FUCKER!"

My anger sparks chain reactions of further fury. I have advanced across the room, and I am looming over his cowering form. My teeth must have elongated as I can no longer form my lips to meet, causing my speech to slur.

"SHAY SHOMETHING YOU SHELFISH P'ICK 'EFORE I 'IP YOUR HEAD OFF YOUR SHOULDERS AND LAUNCH IT AT FUCKIN' KOJAK OVER THERE!"

Unsurprisingly, Pops is frozen in fear. Guess I am significantly scarier than cancer, despite the 'Big C' clocking up a superior number of confirmed kills. I reach forward to grab him, but before I get a grip, I feel a large hand grasp me around the top of my neck and hoist me off my feet into the air.

If I wasn't like I am, this lift would have killed me. Human beings are not designed to be jacked up by the neck. Certainly, no one has survived when I have experimented with it. It's why hanging was a popular choice for executions, it's cheap because you just need a tree, a length of rope and an enthusiastic mob.

A deep voice behind me rumbles, "I see your manners haven't improved much. That's no way to talk to your Dad."

Thursday, 1st October, 22:05

Tak?

Being suspended by the neck means I can't turn around to confirm my suspicion, however Pops doesn't have the same constraints.

"Tak!"

I can see Pops' face positively beaming and warmth is coming off him in waves like a cat being stroked.

"Are you calm Luke? I mean, is it safe to put you down?"

"Yeah."

The shock has evaporated my anger quicker than a puddle in a heat wave. With no perceptible effort, Tak gently lowers me until my feet retake my weight and he releases the pressure on my neck. I turn around not quite believing he's here.

He's eyeing me warily and keeps his attention on me when he asks, "You OK, Pops?"

"You wouldn't believe how pleased I am to see you," he responds.

Pops almost knocks me over as he rushes over to embrace him or, more accurately, Tak hugs him. It only requires one of Tak's huge arms to envelope him and Pops' head only just reaches Tak's chin. It's like Tak is the dad! He still hasn't taken his eyes off mine, like he's expecting me to go for Pops again. Pops disentangles himself (well, Tak lets him go) and he grasps the taller man by the shoulders and looks up at him with tears evident in his eyes. Similar to me, I don't think he truly believes Tak is here. Pops finally lets him go with some clapping of his shoulders like he is checking he is real.

"Let me get you a coffee son and you can tell us what you have been up to all this time. Luke, do you want one?"

I say yes more as a reflex than a concious choice, although my caffeine levels have not changed in the last couple of minutes. Tak has yet to avert his gaze, but I no longer get the impression he's concerned, just intently curious.

"Do I get one?" rumbles Tak.

Despite myself we embrace and, although my feelings are mixed, it feels good.

Tak's my older brother... well not really... well, it's complicated. Strictly speaking he's my cousin. Pops' sister, Aunty Andrea's boy. He came to live with us when he was 13, I was 8. Tak's Stepdad had a wicked temper and thought little of taking it out on Tak. I think he considered him a necessary annoyance who came with Aunty Andrea and was likely counting down the days until Tak's sixteenth birthday, when he could legally throw him out. Pops was a good judge of character, which led to a few altercations with 'Uncle' Bryan. It didn't matter much that Pops was the smaller man. He had no time for bullies, especially those who took it out on women and kids. I think Bryan thought he would be shot of Tak before he could cause him any problems. Bryan was a heavy set 6'2" but at thirteen Tak was tall enough to look his Stepfather in the eye. Bryan had a skin full at the pub. He had come home unexpectedly early and was bawling out Aunty Andrea for not having dinner on the table, even though she had no idea when he would be back. It wasn't the first time Tak had run to his Mum's defence, but it was the first time that Tak had hit him back. He broke Uncle Bryan's jaw in two places. Aunty Andrea jumped to Uncle Bryan's defence and blamed Tak for the whole thing. Tak stormed out of the front door he would never darken again. A couple of hours later he turned up at our house (Tak obviously had never forgotten all the times Pops had stuck up for him) and asked if he could stay. Pops didn't think twice about it. Tak told Pops the whole story and Pops laughed until he cried when he told him the part where he had broke Uncle Bryan's jaw. At the time, I didn't really understand what was going on apart from that I had instantly got a big brother. Tak kept growing and fuelled himself well. Pops used to complain how much Tak cost to feed but it was all a big joke really. Tak stopped growing when his head reached the top of the door frame, but he didn't stop there, just started expanding sideways instead, packing on more muscle until you couldn't tell if a door was shut or if he was just stood in the doorway. He did all the things you would want a big brother to do: played games; took me to the cinema; read stories and; even went to soft play! I never went to B&Q again after Tak came to live with us.

When I was 10, so I guess he was 15, he started going out with a girl called Jane. At first, I was jealous and thought she would take him away from me but, quite the opposite, she adopted me like I was her little brother and, truth be told, she probably hugged me more times than Tak and Pops ever did. If Pops went out of an evening, it was always Tak & Jane who babysat, and I always felt happy & safe.

When I was 20, not long before I transitioned away from my warm life, Tak up and left as suddenly as he'd arrived. Pops said he knew something was up before he disappeared, but Tak wouldn't say what it was. He borrowed some money one evening before he started his night shift (he said he had lost his wallet) and we never saw him again, until tonight. Jane's Dad turned up a few days later, asking if we knew where she was. They had obviously run off together, but no one could fathom why. If she had been pregnant both families would have been pleased as punch. Initially I was furious with Tak for leaving us, especially as he seemed to take an essential part of Pops with him. But not long after my sleep patterns reversed, I became acutely sensitive to daylight and, well, the rest is history.

I am still too stunned to speak so Tak has to break the silence.

"You alrigh'?"

"Depends on your definition of 'Alrigh'."

Tak half smiles at this. Pops comes scuttling back in with three mugs of coffee and a tin of biscuits, the kind you only usually see at Christmas. He plonks them on the coffee table, flavouring the table in his haste. He rips the plastic off which seals the tin and pops off the lid. We all sit, Pops on one sofa and Tak and me on the other. I have to sit forward as there is not enough shoulder room for us both to sit back. That's OK cos I can't take my eyes off him. He's like a ghost from a life past. Pops is sat forward too, all ears, eyes bright.

"So, how are things Tak?"

Pops grabs his knee and squeezes it affectionately but maybe he's thinking the same as me and doublechecking Tak isn't an apparition. Tak's mouth opens slightly but he struggles to find any words, or words he wants to share.

After a pause he says, "You know... can't complain... no ill health or anything like that."

"Kids? Do you have any kids? If they are anything like you, I imagine they are eating you out of house and home," Pops says with a smile, "I nearly had to take out a second mortgage to feed you!"

No pause this time, "No Pops. No kids."

Pops' smile falters as the conversation grinds to another awkward halt.

"What about Jane? How's she doing?"

This question hits home like a punch to the gut a la Mike Tyson. The mother of all pauses follows, and Tak eventually replies.

"She died... she was attacked... she lost too much blood... she died."

Jane died! Even though I hadn't thought about her in years I feel like a part of myself erodes, like a cliff being swallowed by the sea.

"Aw Tak, I'm so sorry son. I didn't see anything in the papers."

"You wouldn't have. We lived a long way from here."

"Is that why you came back? To let us know? When's the funeral?"

"Pops, it was a few years back. There's no funeral to go to."

"Oh."

That knocks the last of out of Pops' enthusiasm, but he still tries his best not to show it. I know during this whole conversation there was one question Pops really wanted to ask, which was, "Why did you go?", but he doesn't want to ask in case that would be enough to spook Tak into making another sharp exit. Pops was trying to stay on safer ground but its seriously backfired. Initially this was the question I wanted to ask, but now I have a more pressing question.

"Tak. Why haven't you aged?"

Thursday, 1st October, 22:33

"The same reason you don't."

Come again? I just guessed the Bonus Catchphrase after only revealing one square. Therefore, I was totally unprepared for the trapdoor that just swallowed me. I fumble about in the dark looking for the cellar door which would lead me back to the most important conversation of my life.

"Huh?" Pops and I exclaim in stereo.

Pops must have been even more surprised than me. He didn't even realise there was a Bonus Catchphrase to solve. Blinded by his joy to have Tak back, he failed to notice his unlined face, grey free hair (cosmetic surgery and hair dye?) but how does someone without superhuman strength grip and lift a grown man off the ground using only the top of his neck as a hand-hold? I listen with purpose and fail to detect a heartbeat.

"It's my fault. I was in such a rush when I left. I literally threw a few things in a bag and left."

Tak's brow furrows as he travels back in time.

"My razor! You must have used my razor!" Tak exclaims.

"So? I always nicked your stuff. Razors, deodorant. I even used your toothbrush once when I accidentally knocked mine into the toilet."

"Christ Luke! How many times did I warn you to leave my stuff alone?"

"I never touched your clothes."

"Only because you would have looked like that kid at the end of that film 'Big'."

There is a warmth in rekindling this old argument. We both smile.

"I should have thrown it out, but I was in such a panic, and I hadn't put all the pieces together by then."

Tak has his face in one of his colossal hands and is massaging his closed eyes.

Pops gets in first, "I don't understand Tak."

"Blood. Contaminated blood. I reckon you only need a trace amount to enter your bloodstream to instigate the transition."

It's too much to take in but thank God for Pops who asks the questions I can't form at the moment, "But, but how did you get er… infected?"

"Well, you know I worked at the hospital?"

"Yeah," Pops replies.

"One of my jobs was disposing of the waste properly. Needles had their own special plastic boxes which meant people like me wouldn't accidentally prick themselves and catch some blood borne pathogen like hepatitis. Well, someone didn't do what they should have done, as a needle ended up in the general waste. When I picked up the rubbish bag, it poked through and jabbed me in the hand. I was up to date with all the vaccinations, but I was still tested to be sure. They all came out negative. They don't test for what we got. Well, I don't need to tell you Luke what happens next. I was doing night shifts, so things like sensitivity to daylight weren't so obvious at first. But the dreams. I tried my best, but it was impossible to ignore the dreams.

They would all start out the same. I'd be doing ordinary, everyday things like making dinner with Pops, or babysitting you Luke (you'd always be young, like the age you were when I first came to stay), or just watching TV on the sofa with Jane. Then something would happen, a trivial disagreement, like Pops would say I was chopping the veg too small, or Luke you'd be cheating at Top Trumps, or Jane would want to watch something different to me on the telly. I'd fly into a fury, nought to sixty in less than a second. More your style than mine Luke. Whoever was in the dream would be petrified and the anger would blend beautifully with my euphoria, like a cocktail. I would hear... feel your elevated heartbeats as clear as a ticking clock in the dead of the night. That's all the prompt I needed to start feasting from your necks (the sound and feel was like biting into a crisp green apple), drinking in the life and screams for mercy in equal measures of pleasure. I would feel everything, but I had no control. As much as I tried to assert it and stop, I couldn't. It was like watching a 4D film. Then I would be me again, all the exhilaration exhausted. Just me, covered in blood. Hugging a mutilated version of one of you, sometimes lifeless but worse still when the body wasn't done spasming with unfocussed, glassy eyes. A disgusting echo of life. Just me, the blood, the guilt and the confusion. Every time I would wake up crying and I started to dread going to sleep in the first place. I would slip into the nightmare within seconds of losing consciousness.

Both Pops & Jane knew something was up, but I didn't know how to even start to explain.

Then the dream happened in real life. Jane couldn't do lies. Maybe it was because her Dad had an affair but, really, I think she was just wired that way. She wouldn't let it go. She knew I wasn't right and, one night before work, she kept digging and digging until I blew my top and the monster took over and I became a passenger. I grabbed a handful of her hair, pulled her head sharply to the left and yanked her opposite arm down hard to provide easy access to her neck. She was crying out in pain but kicking me for all she was worth and digging her nails into the hand which had hold of her hair. I couldn't feel it. It was like a noise in another room. All I could feel was her heartbeat and the exquisite excitement of what was to come. Jane wasn't the only one screaming. Inside, the real me, was shouting myself hoarse to stop. Just like my nightmares, I was impotent, but I kept fighting to break through the glass and regain control. I opened my mouth wide and moved in to gorge. My mouth was so close I could feel her body heat radiating in through it, already starting to replace the cold with warm. Inside I am bellowing 'No!' cos I know it ain't a dream this time.

A miracle happens and I snap out of it. I let go of Jane's hair and she crumples to the floor sobbing, leaving a sizeable clump of her lovely blonde hair in my hand. Her hair becoming detached was the least of her problems. I'd pulled her left arm completely out of the shoulder socket. I'm amazed she lets me near her but all she wants to do is hug and, although I am scared to get close again, that's all I want too. One time at work, one of the A&E doc's showed me how to put a dislocated shoulder back in. She had to bite down on a wooden spoon wrapped in a tea towel, but I managed to do it. She told me my face had changed, like all the kindness and love had ran out like water in a sink and all that was left was a malevolent grin framed by impossibly large canine teeth, sharp as kitchen knives. She said when I let her go my face returned to normal, despite looking like I was taking a desperate breath after a plastic bag was removed from my head.

That's when I decided to run away. I didn't want to hurt her, Pops or you Luke. I had come so close to committing an unforgivable evil. Jane insisted on coming with me. She said she would rather be dead than without me. I told her she probably would end up dead if she came with me. With a determined look she said she was willing to take that chance. I daren't risk another argument so I reluctantly agreed. I came straight here, grabbed some essentials, and pretended I lost my wallet, so we had some extra cash. Sorry Pops.

Jane was waiting in the car, nursing her shoulder. Then we just got onto the motorway and drove like we were being chased, but we weren't going to outrun our problems as we'd packed them. We stopped in the services to buy Jane some painkillers and my new instincts were warning me that sunrise was not far away, so we booked into the adjacent Travelodge. Jane watched over me as I slept through the day. Then we got in the car when the sun went down and just kept going."

I'd fantasised, more times than I could remember, on what I would do to the person responsible for making me this way. I'd barely started to live my own life when it was all stolen and replaced with this car crash. I now know who to point a nuclear warhead's worth of wrath towards, but it turns out to be the only person in the world I love as much as Pops. Who also happens to be the only person who knows, truly knows, what it is like to live with the hunger. I look at Tak and will the rage to bubble up to explosion pressure, but it doesn't happen. All I can see is my reflection.

"So, if it wasn't Jane, why did you come back home son?"

Pops' question snaps Tak and me out of our mutual mesmerisation.

"After the transition, I developed a kind of sixth sense. I can't read minds..."

One nil Lucas.

"....but I can sense things are going to happen before they do."

And the game is all tied.

"I had this feeling I needed to come home. It was like an itch that could only be scratched by acting on it. So, I hit the road and drove all the way back here to find Luke... well... it's probably just as well I got here when I did."

"I'm so pleased you're here Tak. It's a relief to know that Luke won't be on his own when I... when the cancer wins."

Tak gets up and moves in close so that he is face to face with Pops. He is staring him in the eyes, although he appears to be focussing on something beyond Pops' baby blues. Pops seems too surprised to do anything but cooperate. Satisfied, Tak unlocks his gaze and eases himself back on the sofa next to me and I feel my side of the sofa rise up again.

"You have more time than you think old man before that cancer forces you to tap out. You ain't cut from no ordinary cloth Pops."

This makes the 'old man' smile, his eyes more reflective than they should be. He stands, yawns and uses his raising arms as a covert strategy to wipe his eyes.

"Well, that's about all the excitement I can take for one night. I'm bushed." Pops declares.

He squeezes both of our shoulders en route to the stairs and bed.

"I'll see you boys in the mor… I mean tomorrow evening."

"Night Pops," we both chorus like we are 20 and 25 again. Well, I guess in a way, we still are.

Monday, 17th October, 18:57

"Jesus Christ, what are you two up to now?"

Tak & Pops have been as thick as thieves since the prodigal son had returned. You'd think that the old man had only days to live based on the amount of time Tak was spending with him. However, the big guy is insistent that the cancer won't catch up with him until at least a year from now. It's not just the time though, I've been replaced! All the stuff I used to help out Pops with, he's poached now. And the other annoying thing is that he always does things better than I do them. For instance, when they go to the supermarket, Tak drives. Pop's night vision ain't the best but I transitioned before I learnt to drive. No one gives driving lessons at night and what would be the point until driving tests were offered 24 hours a day! When Tak does the clothes washing, he braves Pops' Y-fronts and socks. I wouldn't go near Pops' socks even before I had superhuman levels of smell. When I went to make a coffee, the other day, I had to do a double take on the mug as it looked brand new. Upon scrutinous inspection I confirmed it was my vintage 'Best Son Ever Mug'. Tak had just taken the time to Scotch-Brite the decades of coffee stains out of it. He's a bloody domestic god! Jane must have been treated like royalty! Anyway, back to the present, the dresser doors are wide open and loads of stuff has been pulled out. Please don't tell me Tak has instigated a spring clean! I'll be roped into this.

"Sit down Luke," invites Pops with a joviality which has a permanence that is now starting to irritate, "Tak made you a coffee."

Course he did! I sit down on the unoccupied sofa and find myself surrounded by shoe boxes full of memories. Tak and Pops almost cover everything in coffee, as a find in a decidedly dog-eared box tickles them. Tak passes it over to me with an affectionate smile. It's a photo of me, aged nine I think, dressed in a Tinkerbell outfit and casting a spell with a yellow, battery-operated wand. I fail to see the funny side.

"Grow up you pair of bigots! I was clearly very mature at that age. So much so I wasn't afraid to challenge gender stereotypes."

My soap box speech has the opposite effect and acts as a catalyst for more infantile sniggering.

"I remember that outfit and wand," recalls Pops, "You insisted it was the only thing you wanted from the charity shop that day."

A time capsule appears in Tak's mind that Pops' opens, "Didn't you break that wand hitting your mate Kev over the head with it?"

"He said that fairies were stupid, and that Superman would wipe the floor with Tinkerbell in a fight. Kev came round in his Superman outfit, so he was asking for it really."

"I remember that," says Pops, "Kev's Mum was not happy. Still not sure if it was cos you hit him or because you hit him with a wand dressed as a fairy."

This time the laughter is infectious.

A photo catches my eye and I fish it out of a green, Clarks shoe box. It's Tak and me the first summer the big guy came to live with us. We are soaked to the skin (like we have been in a water fight), brandishing a double scoop Flake 99 each. In the background is a blue sky and the sea and sand of Boscawen beach. Photos are more than glossy printed paper, they are time machines. But I think this story is best told by dipping into Pops' memories.

God it feels good to get out of the car! We left first thing this morning, but it still took the best part of it to get down here! They need to sort out a motorway that runs the length of Cornwall. I stretch out my neck, back, and arms as if someone is pulling my hair and arms back. It doesn't feel like I drove down, more like I had been posted in a small box. Like the car, my tank is empty. Luke, on the other hand, has energy to burn and is bouncing around with excitement like he's on an invisible bouncy castle.

"Can we go to the beach Dad?"

"I wanna get the keys sorted first. Make sure our accommodation is all in order."

Not the meanest words I have ever uttered but they are sharp enough to visibly deflate the little fella.

"I can take him Unc."

I look up at the new addition to our little family. He's only been living with us a few months but it's hard to imagine life before Tak. I don't think my sister took him further than Barry Island and that only happened cos I treated them. Poor kid, he deserves a proper holiday after all the stuff he's been through. Kid? Christ, he's taller and broader than I am! He's only thirteen and he looks like he could slip Luke into his pocket!

"OK. I'll meet you at the ice cream parlour over there in ten minutes and treat you to some ice creams. I shouldn't be long."

I don't get a backwards look as they race to the dune which separates us from the sea. Halfway up the incline I see Tak swing Luke up onto his shoulder. I don't think I could lift Luke with that level of ease. It's been hard to let anyone look after Luke, as it's only been us for so long, and I feel a pull to follow and keep an eye on them. With the exception of Jaws popping up out of the water, I don't think there is much else that Tak couldn't handle. Don't be daft, go get the keys!

It's a one road town so it doesn't take me long to find the small grocery shop where the keys for our apartment are held. I pass our parked-up car on the way to find our accommodation for the week, which is accessed behind a parade of beach side shops. The key to 'Seaspray' is stiff, maybe due to the salty air, but finally yields after a bit of persuasion. There's a bedroom on my right with a bunk bed which I am not one hundred percent sure Tak will fit into. Next to the bedroom is a small bathroom but past that I enter a larger room which, initially, is hard to take in due to the contrast from dark to light. I can see an open plan kitchen diner with a set of open stairs presumably leading to the second bedroom. Maybe the bed up there will be big enough for Tak. I can always bunk with Luke. Plus, I am not sure I'm comfortable sleeping up there whilst the boys are closest to the only way in or out of the apartment. There is a sofa and TV at one end leading onto the sun magnifying patio doors and a balcony beyond. I head straight for the balcony which affords a beautiful view of the cove. It's framed by jagged slate cliffs with tufts of wild green hair. It's low tide which creates a two-tone beach of golden sand crowded with sun worshippers and a mirrored reflection of the sun where the outgoing sea left it's trail. I try to pick out Tak & Luke but it's impossible with so many people and the tide so far out. Despite the distance, the crash of the waves is still audible. The sun warms my face and I take a deep lung full of salty air. Yep, I reckon this is going to be a good holiday. I pick out two figures making their way back up the beach which could be them, or a young dad and his boy. Either way, I shut and lock the patio doors and make my way back out and around to the ice cream parlour which may possibly be sited right underneath our balcony.

It must have been them as we meet outside the ice cream place. However, they are not in the same state as when I last saw them.

"What on earth happened to you two?"

"I never saw that wave coming. The sea at Barry Island was never like that. The Atlantic knocked us over like we were nothing but pebbles, even me," recollects Tak.

"I just remember one minute you were chasing me along the shoreline and the next, I was underwater not knowing which way was up," as I join Tak down memory lane.

Pops' turn, "I remember it took us nearly all holiday to get you to go near the sea after that Luke. But whenever I suggested going anywhere else on holiday, you two wouldn't have it. It had to be Boscawen. Even Jane came when you two got..."

Tak's face darkens and, with the mention of one name, the spell is broken. In lieu of having a real time machine to go back thirty seconds into the past, Pops tries to jump forward into the future to a different space and time.

"I've got to grab some bits from the Co-op."

Tak looks like he has turned to stone and, for the first time since he arrived, he doesn't offer to go with Pops. In a way I'm glad cos it gives me an opportunity to feel useful again.

"Hold up Pops," I call, "A Barry Island wave could you knock you over at the moment and you'll need some muscle to bring those two for one beans home."

Thursday, 29th October, 20:20

"Noooooo!" screams Dani.

"I'm serious, God's honest truth," I reply.

"That was too much to take in. You are going to have to tell me that again."

"Which bit?"

"All of it."

"OK. I was in my last year of GSCE's but not quite sixteen yet. Her name was Mrs. English, which made no sense at all because she taught German. At first, I thought she was just being nice and helping me when I was stuck, which happened a lot because languages ain't my strong suit. However, there are only so many times that she can touch your forearm, talk over your shoulder so close that you feel her warm breath on your neck and her breasts rub up against you while she talks you through the past and present tense before you know it's on purpose. So, when she offered me some private tuition at her house, I had reasonable hopes that we wouldn't be getting any text books out. When she announced we would be watching a German language film to improve my listening skills, my fantasies fell off a cliff. Trying to make the best of it I stuffed my face on the nibbles she had laid out on the coffee table. She turned the lights down low, joined me on the sofa and started the video. It was like watching a low budget soap opera, like those Mexican daytime shows. She asked me if I understood what they were saying. I answered honestly when I said 'a bit'. That made her howl with laughter, not altogether dissimilar to a witch's cackle but lacking in the sinister edge. I think she may have been drinking before I arrived. When she pulled herself back together, she asked me, 'Which bits?' I said I think the blonde lady is saying, 'I'd like it if something happened,' and the brown haired lady is saying something about something being hard. That set her off worse than before. When she recovered, she said, 'Well done. You pretty much got it.' 'Got what?' I thought. I was still load of 'Blankety Blanks' away from understanding what the hell was going on. Then the blonde lady started kissing the brunette lady and I forgot where I was completely. I snapped back to the present when I felt Mrs. English's warm hand on my... well it was somewhere that had only ever been previously explored by my warm hand. Needless to say, this wasn't the last 'catch up session' at Mrs. English's. In fact, it was a regular thing as her husband worked away a lot. I was living every heterosexual teenage boy's fantasy, having sex with an experienced woman more than twice my age. I knew better than to ask her what her actual age was for fear of bursting the bubble. I was the only one in my year who had enough sex to meet the unreasonable demands of teenage hormones. Most boys my age were the equivalent of dogs chasing cars. Like all things it was destined to come to an end sometime and the first sign was when I kept spotting the same strange bloke on the way home from school. You can tell when people are looking at you (it's an instinct) but every time I tried to catch his eye, he looked away. Well, this went on for a couple of weeks (always seeing him on a different stage of the walk) until, not long after I came in from school one day, there was a loud knock at the door. Actually, it was a series of bangs which translated from morse code said, 'Open the door now or I'll bash it the fuck in.' Pops' car wasn't in the drive, so I guess he thought I was home alone. He was half right, Pops' was out. Tak opened the front door, which is the equivalent of opening one door to find another one metre thick steel door directly behind it.

'Can I help you?' rumbled Tak in a voice so full of bass, the gravel in the drive did a little dance.

Silence follows as things have clearly not gone to plan.

'Can I help you?' Tak repeated more slowly in his quiet yet thunderous tone.

In a voice considerably higher than Tak's I heard, 'Where's that little bastard? Tell him to get his arse out here. I want a word with him.'

'Why?' boomed Tak like the voice of God.

In a voice a tiny bit lower than his opening gambit he replied, 'Because the little shit's been fucking my wife. That's fucking why!!'

The words 'Oh Shit' lit up in my mind in big neon lights and my stomach went AWOL, landing somewhere in the cellar. Tak looked back at me, and I saw the faintest hint of a smile. I never told Tak about my 'catch up' lessons in case he told Pops. I had been doing a thorough job protecting my bubble. I had a feeling that this would be the only topic of conversation once this shituation had been navigated.

'Well I'm no marriage counsellor, but I strongly suggest the issue you have is with your wife not my little brother.'

Tak took a step outside of the door then and Mr. English took a hasty step backwards, almost falling on his backside when he stepped back off the doorstep. From the back I could see Tak loosening up his shoulders and neck.

'Now, if I ever see you at this door, or in this street, or if my brother reports back to me he has seen you doing anything other than making a hasty retreat because by some long odds you have accidentally crossed paths, I will take that baseball bat you are holding and perform a magic trick with it and your arse. You're lucky I was in. I wouldn't like to think what Pops would have done to you.'

Pops arrived back within seconds of Mr. English's speedy departure.

With a puzzled look on his face Pops asked, 'Who was that bloke doing a Road Runner impression?'

I had to tell Pops and Tak the whole story then. Pops roared with laughter when Tak told him what happened on the doorstep. Pops said he hoped other door knockers were taking note. He asked me if I had learnt anything. I said, 'Don't get caught next time,' which set him off again. I didn't get in trouble although the 'catch up' lessons ended with immediate effect and Mrs. English was mysteriously ill for the next parent's evening. Pops was disappointed, I think she was the main reason he wanted to go."

"Wow Luke. I didn't think it could be but, that was even better for the second telling."

"It had its downsides besides angry, stalker husbands. It's hard to have meaningful relationships when your benchmark is so messed up. Anyway, I told you that story two times now, so you need to tell me a school story twice as good."

"Well," starts Dani who then takes a deep breath and subsequently downs her double whiskey which is so fresh from the bar the ice cubes haven't started to melt yet, "I was the only girl at an all-boys school."

Bewildered, I can't shield myself from seeing the memory which is at the forefront of Dani's thoughts. I see Dani's twin, disconsolate in a school uniform. Well, he must be an identical twin because, despite the short hair and black trousers, he is the spitting image of her. Except it can't be Dani's twin because she hasn't got one. There'd be other memories of him. So, if Dani has no twin then that must mean the boy is... I wish she hadn't dropped that bombshell when I had a mouthful of cider and black. That's another Egyptian cotton shirt ruined! When you read minds it bloody hard to be blindsided. Her ability to surprise me is clearly not limited to materialising out of thin air! Her light dims as she is transfixed by a very interesting spot in the pattern of the beer-soaked carpet.

"What the fuck?" I manage not one hundred percent sure I am referring to Dani's big reveal or lamenting over the shirt.

She sneaks a look over at me and her mind broadcasts surprise that my seat is still occupied, and I haven't made for the exit.

"I'm Trans."

I feel like the first person told that the world wasn't flat and can't quite wrap my head around the concept. The net result is that I can't find any words. With confusion written all over my face Dani continues to explain.

"Ever since I could remember I never felt comfortable in my own skin. I used to stare at myself naked in the full-length mirror in my parent's bedroom and be convinced the reflection wasn't mine. It was like there had been some kind of mix up when they were putting souls into bodies. Some celestial admin error. There was probably a boy out there with a girl's body who feels exactly the same as I did."

Someone unmuted me, "But you look like a girl! You're Coca-Cola bottle shaped! You even smell like a girl!"

That makes Dani smile a bit.

"I fixed my hormone mix. That helped develop my curves, but my boobs needed an upgrade, so I got implants. I was lucky my Gran left me money in her will to fund it. I wasn't going to do all that and still splash on my grandad's Brut!"

My last comment slipped out with the surprise. I didn't mean whether she has Chanel Number 5 or Old Spice in her bathroom cabinet. I mean she smells like a girl. When you have superhuman smell you can tell the difference.

"Wow. That trumps my story." I concede.

"You're still here?" Dani replies like she is waiting for me to make my excuses.

"Er... yeah... Unlike you, I haven't finished my drink yet."

"You're not put off?"

"Who the fuck I am to judge?"

Did someone just turn the lights on as I feel I am now in the full beam of a search light.

"Drink?" she offers.

"Why not."

Whilst Dani is at the bar a mental jigsaw piece falls into place.

"So, Fish Finger, he knows your secret?"

"Yes... fish... Francis is his real name. We used to be neighbours. Even used to play together when we were very young. He saw me. I was 13 and had just been through a growth spurt which I was very excited about. It meant I was only a fraction shorter than my Mum, which meant I could fit into one of her summer dresses. I was mesmerised by what I saw in the mirror. It felt like the first time I had put on clothes which fitted. Metaphorically speaking, in reality the dress hung off me like it was still on the hanger. I had made a big mistake though. You can feel when someone is looking at you, although you don't usually have that feeling in your Mum and Dad's bedroom. I'd forgotten to close the curtains. From across the road, I could clearly see the wide eyes of Francis followed by a smile that was all teeth and no warmth. Life at school was hell after that. No one wants to be friends with someone with a target that big on their back."

Dani's eyes well up and she looks down again unable to carry on, although I can clearly read the details which are too painful to share. I reach out and cover her hand with mine. She looks up with surprise which causes her full eyes to cascade down her cheeks but her smile returns.

"Can you excuse me for a sec?" asks Dani and I release her hand so she can visit the toilets to sort out the watercolour effect on her mascara.

When she returns her focus is all on me. My eyes drift to her neck, which she misinterprets, which makes her pulse quicken, which only makes things worse.

Her smile is as broad as physically possible when she suggests, "Maybe we can go to my flat? I have an extensive collection of foreign language films."

Every fibre of my being wants to go, and she can see this on my face, but we both have very different agendas.

"I'm sorry Dani. I just remembered I promised I would meet up with Tak."

I can see into her disappointed thoughts that she thinks there are different reasons why I don't want to go back with her. I confirm her belief that she is a disgusting freak, and that this rejection is exactly what she deserves for hoping something would happen. I want to tell her it's not true, but my words would be useless against her 'truth'. She's better off disappointed though than what would have happened as soon as her flat door closed.

"You're going to have to end it with her."

My heart nearly starts again as the alleyway entrance comes to life and steps out onto the pavement. Holy motherfucking midnight! Tak's as good as lurking as I am. Maybe better, seeing as he can eclipse the entirety of an alley mouth.

There's an issue when someone hits upon the truth. The truth is granite hard and anything which hits it bounces back and bludgeons the originator of the strike.

"Fuck off Tak. I am allowed to have a life outside of the Waltons with you and Pops."

"Luke, we need to talk."

"Not interested Tak."

I go for a walk and make sure I come home just before sunrise.

Wednesday, 18th November, 21:00

Overall, I had done a pretty good job avoiding 'the talk' with Tak. A.A. meetings, time with Dani and (as a last resort) more walks up until sunrise. I must buy one of them watches that count your steps. Using Pops as a human shield also worked. It was abundantly clear that Tak did not want to have this conversation in front of him. And so, this game of cat and mouse had played out for weeks.

Horrornation Street had just finished when Pops creakily got to his feet and announced he was popping over the Co-op. A long pause follows as Pops lingers, expecting one of us to offer to go with him. Usually, if there was the shortest of pauses, I would jump in and offer to carry the bags. I rarely got in fast enough as Tak was usually quicker to the punch. I look at Tak quizzically and he deliberately projects an image of him laying flowers upon a grave. The name Jane Stock is engraved in the granite headstone. I get the hint. It must be the anniversary of her death. Pops looks down on us confused as we communicate silently.

"I'll go on me own then," he pouts as he grabs his jacket and heads out into the night.

"Thanks Luke. I can't talk frankly about this with Pops around. He wouldn't understand. I think you are the only person in the world who would."

"Is it true? Is it really the anniversary of her death?"

"It's a few weeks past but you have been particularly hard to pin down."

I don't really want to ask, for fear of the answer, but what choice do I have now?

"What happened?"

"We worked out the triggers pretty quickly. We weren't a break up / make up type of couple so avoiding arguments didn't really require any special effort. It just wasn't in our natures. Jane even learnt meditation to keep her heart rate low. But fear, you know how intoxicating that is."

I am immediately transported through my back catalogue of screaming, crying, pleading women all begging for me to stop. They couldn't have done a better job of egging me on. It was inevitable as soon as they realised I was false advertising. They couldn't stop as much as I couldn't. If someone asked me why I killed all those girls I would honestly answer, "because they begged me to."

"Jane was always a worrier. It came with the package of the wonderful caring person she was. You remember what she was like with you. We never stayed anywhere very long as there would always be some sort of incident. In the best case I would wreck our digs. In the worst case... well the most positive thing I can say is that I didn't kill her. The net result was that we were always in a new environment, living hand to mouth, she was always in fear I would be arrested and that I would go up in flames in a police cell at dawn. As time passed, she started showing signs of age whereas I was immortalised as a twenty five year old, she began to worry that people would notice that too. I told her that she could always pretend to be my Mum, or I could pretend to be a toy boy. Neither of which she found very funny. Anyway, I don't think human beings are designed to cope with being constantly on the run. These little worries grew like seedlings until they were strong vines wrapped around her chest preventing her from taking a breath. The start of the end was when she began having panic attacks, making her heart race and fear to radiate from her in waves. You know that's like a mouse running past a cat, the cat just pounces. It's instinct. I always managed to pull myself back from the brink in time but, Christ Luke, the damage I would do to her before I could regain control. Do you know how hard it is to come to terms with the fact you are responsible for regularly giving the woman you love the beating of her life? I don't think a bruise managed to fade before it was replaced by another. That wasn't even the worst of it. Every time she forgave me. I wanted her to hate me as much as I hated myself. I wanted her to use that hate as fuel and leave. As much as I knew it was the right thing to go, I couldn't bring myself to do it. I wasn't strong enough. She was the strong one, but she used all of that strength to stick by me.

Then one time, Jane has the mother of all panic attacks. I did a lot of door work. I had the look and hours suited my reverse sleep pattern. Plus, people don't tend to ask a lot of questions about your past. It had been the usual sort of night, most people merry but behaving themselves with the occasional threats from people hardly able to stand or just those people you just know in your gut are trouble. For obvious reasons, I never worried about the threats, but some prick had clocked where my car was parked and slashed all my tyres in revenge. No taxis were about at that time in the morning, so I had to walk home. I got home just before sunrise.

Jane was awake and beside herself with worry. She had convinced herself I had been arrested, that I had gone too far with a punter and been hauled off to a police cell with a window view of the east. I don't think police cells even have windows. I tried to calm her down, that it was just a problem with the car (I held back what the problem was) and that I was home now so no need to panic anymore. If only it was as simple as saying the words. She started hyperventilating and her elevated heartbeat found another gear. Her fear for me seamlessly now switched to panic for herself as she felt like she was dying, choking herself of air. She wasn't far from the truth. Her body pulsed in front of me as the backdrop of the flat was eclipsed by her light like a camera flash only more intense. My face changed without me realising it had happened. I grabbed her by her upper arms, sank my fingers deep into her flesh and lifted her into the air. I smashed her into the wall, pinning her like she was nailed to a crucifix before I feasted upon her neck. It was only when her body had no fight in it did my feeding frenzy end. I lowered her to the ground and cradled her whilst blood ran down her shoulder and arm. She lacked the strength, so I helped her to put her hand to my face. She looked deep into my eyes, all the fear replaced with love despite everything. She whispered, "It's not your fault." Her body took on extra weight as it went limp after her heart gave one last weak contraction and then there was nothing in her eyes at all. She used the last of her energy to forgive me. Me, who stole her life, replaced it with a living hell before I ripped her throat out and snuffed out her light. She forgave me even though part of me thought: you deserve this for loving the disgusting thing that I am; you deserve this for insisting on coming with me when I told you not to; you deserve this for all the times I held myself back but didn't want to. Murdering the person I loved most in the world is forever engraved in my memories as the most exquisite moment of my life, because of the taste of her sweet elixir. Do you realise how fucking messed up that is?"

I've killed, more times than I care to remember. I'd be lying to myself if I didn't admit I felt guilty down to my dusty soul. That's why those memories are under such tight lock and key. And those were girls I hardly knew. The guilt debt for someone you love must be next to impossible to bear.

"I couldn't even run away from what I had done. The sun was up by now, so I was forced to keep Jane's mutilated corpse company all day. A large spray of blood now decorated the wall where I had her pinned. I laid her gently in the bath and tried my best to clean up the blood, but you can never get rid of it all, no matter how hard you try. Especially when you have the ability to smell it distinctly. Blood knows it has responsibility to carry guilt. I then had to get myself cleaned up. The hot water steamed up the bathroom mirror, which made it look like Jane was just taking a bath. When I wiped away the condensation there was no mistaking what happened as her head lolled back at a previously impossible angle, presenting the rip in her neck. Every day when I wash my face, I look in the mirror and see her in the bath reminding me there are some things so wicked you can never scrub away the memory."

There follows a pause as Tak reaches the end of being able to share and I reach the end of being able to ignore the truth.

"Okay Tak. I understand. I'll..."

I am interrupted by Pops coming back through the front door. Well, more accurately, Pops falling through the front door.

Wednesday, 18th November, 21:35

We could both smell the blood before we got to him. Tak lifts Pops gently from his face plant and places him into a seated position on the floor, with his back against the wall. Blood is flowing freely from a wound in his side, soaking his clothes. Tak opens up his shirt and places a tea towel against a half inch wide incision. He holds it there, trying to stem the flow, but the towel has already turned red and is starting to drip. Tak seems to know what he is doing, and from what he confided in me, he must have gotten a lot of practice at first aid.

"What happened Pops?" rumbles Tak.

Pops' voice is a whisper, like it's too much effort to talk at a normal volume. Maybe one of his lungs has collapsed. The cut does look deep.

"It all happened so fast. I was on my way back from the Co-op when I noticed a gang of kids. I didn't pay them much attention but one of them stood in my way to ask the time. Before I had chance to answer, they all rushed in to surround me. I thought they were going to try to mug me but then they just all ran away laughing. It was only when I went to take another step did I feel the pain in my side. I think one of them stabbed me, but I don't understand it. I've still got my wallet and keys, they didn't even take my shopping which had some alcohol in it. One of them did say something strange though, when they were jostling me. One of them said, 'tell him Findus Crispy Pancake says hi.'"

"Pops, you need medical attention," advises Tak, "You're bleeding out."

"No hospitals Tak. Better this way."

"Better what way?" I explode, "You're going to hospital."

Tak looks deep into Pops eyes, I think he is dipping into his future again.

"It wouldn't do any good Luke," says Tak in a blank tone, "He wouldn't make it." In a softer tone he addresses Pops, "Do you need anything for the pain?"

"I'm good Tak," says Pops, smiling although even this seems to take some effort, "It's okay as long as I keep still."

I feel like the ground under my feet is falling away. I grip the kitchen counter as my lightheadedness almost causes me to collapse.

"Why the fuck didn't you see this coming Tak?" I say with venom.

Tak doesn't take his eyes off Pops and responds, "I don't come with guarantees. If I did, Jane and I would have lived off lottery wins, not doing crappy jobs and living in flea ridden bedsits. I just knew the cancer wouldn't get him anytime soon."

"Well maybe you are fucking wrong now!"

I advance on Pops with the intent of throwing Tak aside and hauling the old man off to A&E. Tak doesn't move from his crouched position, back to me, holding in Pops' side.

He speaks like a faraway roll of thunder warns of lightning, "Try and move me and I will put you through the fucking wall."

"But we have to do something!" I wail frantically.

"Do what Luke? He's gone."

"What?"

I reach out to touch Pops thoughts, something I have done every day since I departed my warm life, but there's nothing to grasp for. I feel like I am drifting out into open sea with no motor or anchor. I suddenly feel like I need air again but can't take a breath. Panic swamps me. My head is misfiring all over the place. Gravity finally wins as my legs buckle and I fall, fall in time, back to 1987.

Where's my Daddy? Where's my Daddy gone? He told me it would be busy and that I needed to keep close so I wouldn't get lost. But I dropped my Matchbox Car and it rolled in the opposite direction and, after I caught it, I turned round and he was gone. Swallowed by the constantly changing mass of giant-sized adults in the shopping arcade. It's all my fault, he told me not to bring it, but I snuck it into my pocket anyway. He's going to be so angry if he ever finds me. But how could he ever see me through this wall of bodies, all at least twice my size? It's just like he said, I am lost forever now! My head starts to swim, and my legs can no longer support my weight. My back slides down the shop window and I collapse onto its low and narrow ledge. The seething mass of shoppers looks even bigger now and look like they are moving faster from down here. The world goes watercolour, and my throat constricts as the hopelessness turns to tears. Tears that will never stop and I bury my head in my folded arms, so I don't have to see anymore.

I open my eyes and I am back in present, which is worse than the memory, although it has been a long time since I was capable of tears.

Tak gets up and stares at his bloodied hand. I don't need to dip into his thoughts to know what he is reliving. He looks down at the shrivelled husk that was Pops. It almost seems impossible that he inhabited that body only minutes before.

There's a liquid nitrogen coldness to Tak's voice when he asks, "Did you manage to dip into his thoughts before he went Luke? I mean, did you see who did this to him."

I speak, although I still feel far away, like I am underwater, "No, but I didn't need to. I know who did this. He must have seen us together on the trip back from the Co-op the other night. I thought he might go after Dani, but not Pops. In fact, I'd forgotten all about him."

"Findus Crispy Pancake? I thought he was delirious."

"No, Fish Finger."

"Fish Finger? Seriously? And do you know where to find... Fish Finger?"

"He's got his own bus stop although I think Thor has dibs on it too."

"Are you alright Luke? Did you bang your head when you fell?"

I get up, a sense of purpose brings me back to my body which starts to swell with a newly tapped source of rage that feels limitless. I didn't lose Pops this time, he was taken.

"I think I've worked out something we can do."

"Good," replies Tak, "I think we need to go and punch someone's ticket."

Tak follows me out the door slamming it so hard on his way out that a load of roof tiles dislodge and fall, smashing on the drive.

There are twelve of them in all gathered at Thor's bus stop, mostly lads but there are a couple girls too. All laughing and joking, smoking, drinking Co-op own brand cider. It looks like a victory celebration. Personally, I think it's premature. One of his cronies gives Fish Finger a nudge when he sees me approach. He flicks his smoke away and smiles widely, like he was welcoming an old friend. The rest of the group don't appear threatened by me advancing but start to look more concerned about the shadowy mountain following behind.

I have the advantage over Tak as I know which of these waste of space cunts is Fish Finger. I head straight for him, resuming my position in his personal space, nose to nose pre-fight style, exactly where I was when Dani led me away. I clearly hear his switchblade spring its knife. He must have cleaned it but I could still distinctly smell Pops' blood on it. I could have easily stepped aside, or stopped his thrust which caused the blade to travel through the inside of my ribcage and puncture my heart. I collapse on the floor, and I can hear the triumph in Fish Finger's mind. This is what happens to motherfuckers who disrespect him and, better than telling the story, he's done this in front of his gang. He has proven without doubt that he is top dog.

"Will you stop fucking about Luke," growls Tak.

The incision in my heart has already healed although the rest of the puncture may need some assistance. I'm not messing about though. I want this fuckface to fall from the highest point possible and right now this is the pinnacle of his sad existence. To his amazement I jump to my feet like I have merely slipped on a banana peel. He moves to stick me again, but I catch his wrist and snap it which makes a crack which is surprisingly loud with little background noise to muffle it. My hand covers his mouth quickly to stifle his cry. I give his wrist a further squeeze, although only myself and Tak can hear the broken ends of the bone splinter. My hand over his mouth continues to do a good job of keeping his screams private.

I move in closer and whisper in his ear, "This is for Pops & Dani but mostly Pops."

I release Fish Finger's mouth and he tries to say 'Sorry' but is cut off as my fist connects with his yellow teeth. My knuckles exit the back of his skull causing blood, brain and teeth to pebble dash the plexiglass behind. That's when the screaming starts. Young men screaming at the same pitch as primary school kids in the playground at break. I struggle to get my hand back through the hole in Fish Finger's head, so we look like some sort of extreme ventriloquist act which I think adds to the hysteria. Tak goes to work butchering the rest of the gang. Dismembering arms and legs and twisting heads off necks so that bodies become bloody roman candles. He crushes heads using only one of his huge mitts, and they explode like dropped watermelons. Others are thrown against the back of the bus shelter, like it was the ropes on a wrestling ring except they don't bounce back, their spines splintering on impact. I finally manage to extricate my hand from Fish Finger's skull and subsequently catch one of the skanky girls who tries to make a break from Tak's rage past me. I rip a hole in her neck and drink. She tastes rank, and her light is dim, but she's a necessity and I need her to heal. Tak and I hunt down the only one of the twelve who has successfully escaped the scene. I sniff him out hiding in a privet hedge and drag him back by his hair. I experiment to see if I can break the plexiglass with his face. It doesn't work but it does turn it into a flat mess before he dies of shock. When we have finished, Thor's Bus Stop is painted with so much red that it continually drips blood from under the roof.

"Come on, I know where Fish Finger's parents live," I indicate to Tak turning my back on Thor's bus stop.

Tak grabs my arm.

"No Luke, this is enough."

I look over my shoulder at Tak, bearing my elongated teeth, "It will never be enough," I hiss.

"Maybe, but it's enough for now."

His grip on my arm is unyielding and to break free from it would probably mean detaching my arm at the shoulder. I begrudgingly follow him back towards the house. We arrive back less than ten minutes after the roof tiles smashed out the front. We are both monochrome like we bathed in the blood of our enemies but, in reality, it was more like a shower with Thor's bus stop providing an effective shower screen. We take a sofa each and sit down.

There's a pause before Tak asks, "Want a coffee Luke?"

"Why not?" I reply.

We sit there in silence until our undrunk coffees are cold. Tak eventually breaks the silence.

"Do you want to go to the beach?"

Wednesday, 18th November, 22:07

Tak didn't mean Barry Island. He meant Boscawen! In Cornwall!

When you are most active at night and most places are shut, the sun does worse than skin cancer and, you are just trying to make it until the next sunrise without murdering a girl, holidays are not high on the list of priorities. Plus, I hadn't left Cardiff since the transition, which kind of made the city limits the edge of the world. If Tak had made this suggestion forty-eight hours earlier, I probably would have freaked out at the thought. I look over at Pops' deflated body which looks nothing like him now that his essence has gone. He looks like some random tramp we found on the way home and dumped near the front door. I look around the room which should look homely and familiar but now, like Pops, looks alien. Without him, it's now just a house. The world's changed. It's no longer a hard decision.

"Fuck it. Let's do it."

As much as I would have liked to, we couldn't just jump in the car and go. Two grown men covered in the blood of a dozen teenage dirtbags is likely to draw attention on a long road trip to Cornwall. We debated what to do with Pops' body. I was all for torching the house like a viking burial at sea. It seemed fitting for a man who spent the majority of his life never taking a backward step. Tak sensibly pointed out the flaws in this poetic approach. Namely the police interest in a car registered at an address which was going up in flames, or a charred stain on the ground. If we were going to make it to our destination before sunrise, we didn't have time to bury him. We even toyed with the idea of taking him with us ('Weekend at Bernie's' style, except he'd be in the boot not riding shotgun) but again not worth the risk if we got pulled over. Leaving the body where it was would be the quickest and easiest solution but may get the attention of the postman when he started to rot. In the end we decided to defer the decision and put his body in the 'spare' freezer. This chest freezer had never seen a fish finger, or a Findus Crispy Pancake, but had seen more than one dead body in its time. We'd work out what to do with him when we got back. I'd seen a programme once where people did this with their dead pets. The pets never made it out of the freezer as the owners could not bring themselves to deal with the grief that the finality of a cremation or a burial would bring. Tak cleaned up the pool of blood (well he did used to be a cleaner) while I carried Pops down the cellar stairs.

I had to cross his arms to be able to close the lid of the freezer. He looked like a vampire in his coffin, with built in special effects as the cold condensed with the warmer air creating a rolling mist. I smile at the irony before kissing his forehead and closing the door.

After depleting a full bottle of shower gel each, we are presentable and ready to roll. A couple of minutes later we come to a stop at the lights outside the Co-op. I look over to the shop front where I can see Dani working the till, shining brighter than the fluorescent lights of the store ever could. Tak notices me looking her way.

"Do you want to speak to her before we go?"

I pause, not sure.

"No. Let's go."

The lights change and we pull away. I swear she looks up and sees us as we drive off and I wonder if I made the right call.

We drive in silence for a while, lost in our own thoughts or maybe numbing them. Even with advanced night vision it's difficult to pick out any landmarks en route. The only way I can tell how far we have gone is from the road signs for motorway exits.

On the M5 just past the turn off for Clevedon Tak asks, "Have you ever met anyone like us?"

I am sure of my answer but then I remember something which makes me revise, "Well not exactly. I did meet a guy in a bar once who had a golden lizard inside him."

"A killing machine? Like us?"

"Well, the guy shone like a saint, but the lizard was as dark as he was light, but he seemed to have it well under control."

"Cos of the amount of times Jane and I had to move on, we pretty much travelled the length and breadth of Britain.

Although I met some dark souls along the way, but I never saw anything like us."

Tak pauses before he asks, "Luke, what do you see when you look at me?"

I turn and look at him perplexed.

"Don't look at me using your memory of me," Tak continues, "Look at me properly, with your hunting eyes."

I know what he means although I don't usually have to think about it. It's the focus that sees beyond the physical and perceives the beauty of someone's inner light. The life force that we crave. This luminescence emanates from everyone in lesser, or larger, degrees. Some people, like Dani, shine so bright that it is like looking directly into the sun. Looking at Tak is like peering into a black hole, a place where all light is consumed, and none can escape.

"Can you see it?" asks Tak.

"See what Tak? You're a fucking eclipse man. No wait. I can see something."

At his core I can see a tiny, flickering light. Although Tak is only a few inches away it looks like I would have to travel for hours to reach that light. Like someone has dropped a match in the middle of nowhere, a dying flicker in the dark.

"I can see a tiny light but it's so small that I keep losing track of it."

"Do you know what that is Luke?"

I have a pretty good idea but find myself not wanting to say. If I don't say, then maybe I can prevent it from being real. So, I play dumb.

"Nope. What is it?"

"I think that light is the last of my humanity. That light gets dimmer every day, as I drift further from the man I was. What happens when the dark envelopes it and the light goes out for good? What on earth is going to stop us from rampaging through this world?"

I don't answer as the question is clearly rhetorical.

"Do you know what I see when I look at you?"

I answer quickly and honestly in that I don't want to know, "No."

Tak spares me but I can't help dipping into his thoughts and see the ugly mirrored truth. I turn on the radio for no other reason than to ensure that Tak does not continue this conversation. He thankfully takes the hint and returns his full attention to the sparsely populated motorway, doing a great job at keeping the needle steady at the seventy miles per hour marker.

At Exeter, we merge onto the A30 and the road narrows. Three notes unmistakeably announce the start of the James Bond theme 'Goldfinger' from the car speakers. A thought occurs to me before Shirley makes her grand entrance. Having possession of the volume gives me the only means possible to sing over her weapon of a voice.

"F-ish-fingerr!" I warble,

"He's the man, the man who messed with Pops

So we redecorated his bus stop."

Tak snorts as he tries to contain a laugh.

"Such a c-o-l-d finger!"

We both crack up then and Tak has to correct his steering to prevent us leaving the A30 between exits.

Just past 1 A.M., we leave the A30 and head south onto the narrow country lanes which lead to Boscawen. When we reach the top of the cliff road, which peers into the cove, it triggers echoes of the excitement I felt as a kid every time we arrived here. The road drops steeply, like a roller coaster, before a sharp bend to the right, then a right again to turn into the resort. We pass some lightless houses (including the one which inexplicably has a turret!), the small grocery and fish & chip shops before reaching the dunes to the left and the empty car park on the right.

We get out of the car, stretch and I could be a kid again. It doesn't matter that it's pitch black. It doesn't matter the place is a ghost town. The ghosts here manifest the happiest times of my life. Without even dipping into Tak's thoughts, I know he is feeling the same. All bittersweet memories as every one of them involve Pops or Jane.

Without saying a word, I break into a sprint toward the beach. Tak is only caught fractionally off guard, and I feel the ground shake as he gives chase. Christ! He moves quick for such a big guy. We instantly time travel.

It's a sunny day, we've just arrived and Tak, me and Pops are all racing toward the shoreline. It's hard going on the soft, dry sand and we need to navigate some families camped out on the beach but, when we reach the compact wet sand of the recently retreated tide, we are all running flat out. Well, I am anyway. I feel like I am flying, and my feet are only touching the sand to ensure that I don't take off into the sky. The sea air is blowing through every hair on my head, arms and legs. My heart is pumping in time with my piston like legs. I have never felt more alive. I am going to beat Tak and Pops this time, I am sure of it. Tak and I stretch ahead and moments later we hit the finish line in the shallow water of the waves. It's a dead heat. I suspect Tak slowed up to make sure we drew but I don't care. I'm too exhilarated to care. Pops is catching his breath just short of the waves, trying to do the impossible, to laugh and take a breath in at the same time. I look up at Tak who flashes me a smile and a knowing wink.

I look back at Pops but see nothing but darkness. The spell is broken, and we are wrenched back into the cold present. I look back at Tak and I can still see his wide grin reflect in the moonlight.

We trudge back up the beach, our squelching shoes betraying our location in the black. At the top of the beach Tak inclines his head toward the cliff path. I nod and we trek to the top. At the summit we park ourselves on a familiar bench which looks out over the Atlantic.

"I'm so sorry Luke. I can't put into words how sorry I am."

"Sorry for what Tak? Coming here was a great idea. That was awesome!"

"No Luke. I'm sorry what I did to Jane, what I did to you, sorry I left, the knock-on effect it had on Pops. I'm so, so sorry. I destroyed all your lives."

If Tak was still capable of crying, I'm sure he would be right now. I don't say anything to begin with as I don't know what to say. He's right. My life was royally fucked up and Pops came along for the ride. I think Tak is asking himself the wrong question though.

"Tak man. You didn't intend any of this. You couldn't build a better big brother than you even with a computer."

I can feel that Tak takes some comfort in the words despite not changing his opinion on his personal responsibility.

"You are right about one thing Luke. This isn't my machination. Someone... something did this to us. We are like two starving wolves air dropped into a field of sheep. We've been set up to kill, and keep killing, with no boundaries put upon us, bar daylight. We are some sort of sick joke, gods with no free will. Our humanity is holding on by a thread before we tear through this world. I am not going to be controlled anymore Luke."

"Tak. Why did you bring me here? Real reason?"

"I know you've looked."

"I know you know. I need you to say it."

"Let's finish it here. Let's use the last of our free will and make a choice before we don't have any left."

I look toward the horizon, where the sun will rise in a few hours' time.

"What about Pops?" I ask.

"Luke, how many people have you killed?"

"Err, I think I'll decline to answer that."

"Point is, was any remnant of that person left after you had finished with them or were they just all empty bottles? What's left in that freezer aint Pops."

There follows a silence as I consider Tak's words.

"Do you have a mobile?" I ask.

"Yep. I bought a 'Pay As You Go' one in the shop at the services."

It takes me longer than it should to write the text but only because I am not used to using mobile phones. I do know her number by heart though, the only one I know apart from my home number.

> I WISH THINGS COULD HAVE BEEN DIFFERENT. LUKE.

I pass the phone back to Tak.

"Did it send?"

"Yep." replies Tak before standing up and launching the phone out to sea. In the dark, it looks like the phone reaches the horizon before it splashes down and sinks. Must be a trick of the light or, more accurately, a trick of the dark.

We spend the rest of the night reminiscing. The dawn could have been many more hours away and we could have easily filled the time with happy stories and memories of Boscawen starring Pops, me, Jane and Tak.

The paranoid fear which precedes the dawn hits us simultaneously. We both fight the urge to flee the bench and frantically dig a hole to hide from the sun. The sky has lightened now, and I am shaking as my instincts scream that the sun is about to appear from the edge of the ocean. I grab Tak's hand and he squeezes mine back. I can feel him shaking too.

I surprise myself when I say, "I love you Tak."

He glances my way briefly, before returning his eyes to the imminent doom on the horizon, and replies, "I love you too little bro."

To my amazement, the searing pain doesn't come. It's just warm, pleasantly warm like getting into a bath. It's the first warmth I have felt since the time my lungs needed air and my heart wasn't a rock in my chest. The warm travels up my legs and my torso. When it finally reaches my eyes all I can see is light. Bright, white, beautiful light.

Acknowledgements

As usual none of what I write is possible without the help of the people in my life. Big thanks to my wife Sam and our friend Esther for your comments on the early drafts of this story. Thanks as well to Brandon, Sean, Anne-Marie and Jelly who read early versions of Lucas, your positive comments meant a lot. And special thanks to my friend Fliss who could see past the inprecise dialogue of Dani, saw the intent of what I was trying to say and helped me find the words so that what she said rang true. I truly could not of finished this book without your help.

For those of you who want to find out more about Tyler and his golden Lizard, check out 'Midas'
also available on amazon.

Printed in Poland
by Amazon Fulfillment
Poland Sp. z o.o., Wrocław
12 January 2023

e6c893f2-8e63-41d1-b030-a2d4bce294a3R01